Hot Stories for Cold Nights

Berkley Heat titles by Joan Elizabeth Lloyd

NAUGHTY BEDTIME STORIES
BAWDY BEDTIME STORIES
THE SPICY BEDTIME COMPANION
HOT STORIES FOR COLD NIGHTS

Hot Stories

for Cold Nights

ALL-NEW EROTIC TALES TO BRING
THE HEAT BETWEEN THE SHEETS

JOAN ELIZABETH LLOYD

HEAT | NEW YORK

THE BERKLEY PUBLISHING GROUP
Published by the Penguin Group
Penguin Group (USA) Inc.
375 Hudson Street, New York, New York 10014, USA
Penguin Group (Canada), 90 Eglinton Avenue East, Suite 700, Toronto, Ontario M4P 2Y3, Canada
(a division of Pearson Penguin Canada Inc.)
Penguin Books Ltd., 80 Strand, London WC2R 0RL, England
Penguin Group Ireland, 25 St. Stephen's Green, Dublin 2, Ireland (a division of Penguin Books Ltd.)
Penguin Group (Australia), 250 Camberwell Road, Camberwell, Victoria 3124, Australia
(a division of Pearson Australia Group Pty. Ltd.)
Penguin Books India Pvt. Ltd., 11 Community Centre, Panchsheel Park, New Delhi—110 017, India
Penguin Group (NZ), 67 Apollo Drive, Rosedale, North Shore 0632, New Zealand
(a division of Pearson New Zealand Ltd.)
Penguin Books (South Africa) (Pty.) Ltd., 24 Sturdee Avenue, Rosebank, Johannesburg 2196,
South Africa

Penguin Books Ltd., Registered Offices: 80 Strand, London WC2R 0RL, England

This book is an original publication of The Berkley Publishing Group.

This is a work of fiction. Names, characters, places, and incidents either are the product of the author's imagination or are used fictitiously, and any resemblance to actual persons, living or dead, business establishments, events, or locales is entirely coincidental. The publisher does not have any control over and does not assume any responsibility for author or third-party websites or their content.

PRINTING HISTORY
Heat trade paperback edition / October 2010

Library of Congress Cataloging-in-Publication Data

Lloyd, Joan Elizabeth.
Hot stories for cold nights / Joan Elizabeth Lloyd.—Heat trade pbk. ed.
   p. cm.
ISBN 978-0-425-23527-0
1. Erotic stories, American.   I. Title.
PS3562.L72H675 2010
813'.54—dc22

2010013194

PRINTED IN THE UNITED STATES OF AMERICA

10 9 8 7 6 5 4 3 2 1

Contents

Contents

*Welcome to my latest collection of deliciou[...]
enjoy reading most of them as much as I en[...]
said most, not all. Some you might find are[...]
particularly in erotic writing, is so varied[...]
fore, if you find a story that doesn't curl yo[...]*

As you read, you'll notice a few things.[...]

*First, there are many tales centering on [...]
to try some new adventure in the bedroom o[...]
are creative ideas there, activities you and[...]
attempt. Go for it. Give a story to your par[...]
a "Honey, how about this for an idea?" Yo[...]
can spice up your love life by delving into so[...]*

*Second, you'll probably spot several simil[...]
theme. Be careful what you wish for. Or [...]
what you are and what you have. Think abo[...]*

Okay, enough of me, let's get to the tales.[...]

Hot Stories for Cold Nights

Leprechaun Love

"*That* must be him," Pete heard his wife, Missy, yell. "Catch him!"

Pete was puffing, running close enough to the leprechaun to almost but not quite grab him. He didn't have enough breath to answer his wife.

Half an hour earlier, he had picked Missy up after she'd gotten off from work and they had started to drive home. Then the sky had darkened and rain had fallen, accompanied by a few halfhearted rolls of thunder and a couple lightning flashes. Then, as suddenly as it had begun, the rain had stopped, the sun had come out, and a magnificent rainbow had filled the eastern sky. It had been so bright that there had even been a perfect rainbow below, the colors in the opposite order.

"That is soooo gorgeous," Missy had said. "And maybe this one will have a leprechaun with a pot of gold at the end."

"Fat chance," Pete had answered. "We're not that lucky."

"I've seen articles in the paper about folks who've caught leprechauns. One said a woman ended up with a condo."

"Yeah, I read that, too, but most folks just get a lottery ticket. And most of them are losers."

Missy had pointed toward a nearby park. "The end looks like it's just over there in Franklin Park. Let's give it a try."

With no real plans, Pete had driven into the parking lot and pulled into a space. "What have we got to lose? Anyway, it's a nice evening for a walk."

Then they had seen him, a short guy all dressed in green. Tight, short green pants, a white shirt with a kelly green vest and a silly bright green top hat. He had spotted them and grinned. Then he'd taken off. The chase was on.

They'd run across half the park it seemed, but now Pete thought that the leprechaun was slowing down. *Maybe he's as exhausted as I am.* "I can't believe we might actually catch him," Missy said from about fifty feet behind. *What "we"?* Pete thought.

Almost totally out of energy, Pete took one last chance and lunged at the little man. Surprised, he felt cloth. That was an amazing piece of luck. He hadn't realized that he was quite that close. Pete dropped to the ground and yanked. The little man tumbled onto the grass beside him, panting.

Missy ran up and quickly wrapped her hand around the

Contents

CONTENTS

Welcome to my latest collection of delicious short stories. I know you'll enjoy reading most of them as much as I enjoyed writing them. Notice I said most, not all. Some you might find aren't to your taste, since taste, particularly in erotic writing, is so varied and so very personal. Therefore, if you find a story that doesn't curl your toes, move on to another.

As you read, you'll notice a few things.

First, there are many tales centering on folks just like you, who want to try some new adventure in the bedroom or outside of it. Perhaps there are creative ideas there, activities you and your partner might like to attempt. Go for it. Give a story to your partner as a suggestion, sort of a "Honey, how about this for an idea?" You'll be amazed at how you can spice up your love life by delving into someone else's.

Second, you'll probably spot several similar stories, all with the same theme. Be careful what you wish for. Or maybe better put, treasure what you are and what you have. Think about it.

Okay, enough of me, let's get to the tales. Enjoy!

—Joan Elizabeth Lloyd
joanelloyd@att.net

Hot Stories for Cold Nights

Leprechaun Love

"*That* must be him," Pete heard his wife, Missy, yell. "Catch him!"

Pete was puffing, running close enough to the leprechaun to almost but not quite grab him. He didn't have enough breath to answer his wife.

Half an hour earlier, he had picked Missy up after she'd gotten off from work and they had started to drive home. Then the sky had darkened and rain had fallen, accompanied by a few halfhearted rolls of thunder and a couple lightning flashes. Then, as suddenly as it had begun, the rain had stopped, the sun had come out, and a magnificent rainbow had filled the eastern sky. It had been so bright that there had even been a perfect rainbow below, the colors in the opposite order.

"That is soooo gorgeous," Missy had said. "And maybe this one will have a leprechaun with a pot of gold at the end."

"Fat chance," Pete had answered. "We're not that lucky."

"I've seen articles in the paper about folks who've caught leprechauns. One said a woman ended up with a condo."

"Yeah, I read that, too, but most folks just get a lottery ticket. And most of them are losers."

Missy had pointed toward a nearby park. "The end looks like it's just over there in Franklin Park. Let's give it a try."

With no real plans, Pete had driven into the parking lot and pulled into a space. "What have we got to lose? Anyway, it's a nice evening for a walk."

Then they had seen him, a short guy all dressed in green. Tight, short green pants, a white shirt with a kelly green vest and a silly bright green top hat. He had spotted them and grinned. Then he'd taken off. The chase was on.

They'd run across half the park it seemed, but now Pete thought that the leprechaun was slowing down. *Maybe he's as exhausted as I am.* "I can't believe we might actually catch him," Missy said from about fifty feet behind. *What "we"?* Pete thought.

Almost totally out of energy, Pete took one last chance and lunged at the little man. Surprised, he felt cloth. That was an amazing piece of luck. He hadn't realized that he was quite that close. Pete dropped to the ground and yanked. The little man tumbled onto the grass beside him, panting.

Missy ran up and quickly wrapped her hand around the

man's wrist. The three took a few moments to calm down. Finally, his heartbeat now more normal, Pete looked at Missy and said, "Now what?"

She dropped to the grass beside the other two, still holding the little guy's arm. "Now," she said to the leprechaun, "you give us your gold."

His giggle was high-pitched. "No gold." He cleared his throat. "Sorry, no gold."

"We caught you fair and square. You've got to give us your gold," Pete said.

"Got no gold," the little man said.

"I read about that in that Internet article," Missy said to Pete. "Some leprechauns don't have gold. That's how the woman ended up with the condo. Somehow, the leprechaun made it happen."

"How do we know he's telling the truth?"

"He has to as long as we've got him." She brandished the little man's arm, still in her grasp.

"That's right," he singsonged. "I'll tell the truth."

Pete sighed. "Okay. No gold. What do you have?"

"Wisdom," the leprechaun said. "Wisdom that will make you famous and wealthy. Most of all, wisdom that will make you happy."

"Okay," Pete said warily, "like what?"

"Good sex," he said.

"Right," Missy responded sarcastically. "Good sex."

"Great sex, actually."

"Our sex life is just fine the way it is," Pete said. "What else have you got?"

More leprechaun giggles. "Nothing else. Nothing else."

"You know, Pete, he might have a point. There might be things we could learn."

Pete stared at his wife. "Are you saying that our sex life isn't any good?"

"Not at all," Missy said, swiftly backpedaling. "But there's always new stuff. I read lots of tips in magazines. Maybe we could spice things up a little."

"I can give you that," the leprechaun said. "Right here, right now."

"Right here? In the middle of the park? In public?" Pete gasped. Actually the idea of making out in the open air appealed to him.

"No one's around. This place is really private. No one comes here." The leprechaun giggled. "Actually, *comes here* is a great choice of words." He winked. "Wanna? Come here, I mean."

The couple thought for a few moments, then Pete said, "What do you think, Missy? You say there are things we could do better. I could . . ." This was so silly. He was content with their sex life. He loved his wife and loved having sex with her. If she wasn't totally satisfied, however, he was willing to give this a try. In the open air. Yeah.

"Would you really?" Missy said. "I mean, don't get me wrong . . ."

"Okay," the leprechaun said, "stop the mental gymnastics and let's get on with it. I've got places to be and things to do that don't involve you." He shook his arm, still in Missy's grasp. "You'll have to let go, though."

"Can we trust you?" she replied. "Once I've let go . . ."

"Let go!" he snapped. "A promise is a promise."

Pete was a little surprised to discover that he was actually getting more than a little aroused thinking about doing it here, especially with the little guy watching.

Missy let go of the man's arm.

"Okay," he said in his high-pitched voice. "It all starts with kissing."

"Kissing? We kiss okay," Pete said.

"Well," Missy said. "I wouldn't mind more really good kissing." She propped herself on her elbow and looked down at her husband. "You mean like this?" she said. She lightly brushed his mouth with hers. Concentrating on his lips, she teased, nibbling on his lower lip and licking.

"That's not bad," the leprechaun said. "Pete, what about you?"

Pete realized that he was totally enjoying the feel of Missy's lips against his. He rolled so he was leaning over her now and kissed her with as much passion as she'd shown.

"Nice," the leprechaun said. "Real nice."

The sound of the little fellow's voice aroused Pete. He was watching them kiss. Would he watch them go further? He pressed his tongue against Missy's lips and she opened her mouth. As he invaded, his hand stroked her shoulder and arms, eventually venturing to her breast. Was the guy still watching?

"Nice," he purred softly. "Yes, just like that."

Pete played with Missy's breast through her T-shirt and bra and heard both Missy and the leprechaun sigh.

Finally, Pete said, "Okay, leprechaun, what now?"

"What do you want now, Missy?" he asked.

Missy wriggled beneath Pete and managed to pull off her T-shirt. "More," she said, slightly breathless.

Her bra was pink lace and Pete's fingers found her already swollen nipple through the fabric. He knew how she liked to have her buds played with and he rolled it between his fingers.

"Like that, Missy?" the leprechaun asked.

"Maybe not so hard."

Okay, Pete thought, easing his touch, and pulling slightly. "Like this?"

"Oh, yeah," she said, her hips beginning to move beneath him.

"What about a little sucking?" the leprechaun suggested. "Do you enjoy things like that, Missy?"

"Mmm" was Missy's affirmative reply.

"This way?" Pete said, drawing one turgid nipple into his mouth, wetting the fabric of her bra.

"Oh, yeah," she purred.

"Maybe without the bra now," the little man said.

"Yes," Missy moaned, lifting her shoulders and unclipping the hooks. "Suck me good."

This was new. Missy wasn't usually aggressive in bed, and she seldom said things like that. Pete felt his cock hardening as he fastened his mouth on her breast.

"Suck harder," she said. When he complied, she said, "More. Bite me a little."

If that's what she wants, that's what she'll get, Pete thought. He carefully used his teeth, but she grabbed the back of his head and tangled her fingers in his hair, guiding his mouth to where she wanted it. "Now the other," she said, her breath now coming in short bursts.

She twisted so he could get a better angle as he licked, sucked, and bit her other tit. "She's got great tits," the leprechaun said, and Pete felt her body jerk.

"You tell me," she said to her husband.

"You've got beautiful tits," Pete said, torn between arousal and surprise that she enjoyed hearing words like that. "I love sucking them." He could feel her excitement rising as he spoke.

"How about giving him some?" the leprechaun said. "His cock needs attention."

"Does your cock need attention?"

Pete's heat was rising to the boiling point. "God, yes," he moaned.

She reached between them and squeezed his hard erection through his pants.

"Too many clothes," the little man said. "Time to strip."

The couple quickly removed their clothing, too hot to even think about the small man watching and directing their actions. "And it's time to finger her," he said, cackling.

Pete slipped his hand down Missy's belly and combed through her pubic hair until he found her erect clit. She was so wet that he could easily stroke her and feel her entire body react.

"Is he doing a good job?" the leprechaun asked.

"A little softer," she said. "I like long, slow, soft strokes right now."

Pete obliged, understanding exactly what his wife wanted.

"And you, young lady, grab his cock. It needs some rubbing."

Missy wrapped her fingers around his cock and stroked along its length. "Squeeze harder," Pete said, "and move your hand a little faster."

"Put your finger inside me." She moaned as she stroked him exactly the way he stroked himself when he jerked off.

He slid one finger into his wife's sopping hole. "Another," she cried, almost screaming in her need. "I need more. Fill me up!"

He did as she asked and felt her channel muscles clench on his fingers. He could wait no longer. Pete moved between her legs and plunged into her, driving his hard dick deeper and deeper.

"Yes," she screamed, "like that. Now harder. Fuck me harder. I'm going to come. Right. Now!"

She screamed as her legs twined around his hips and she thrust her hips upward.

His orgasm followed in just a few moments.

Missy and Pete dozed on the grass until the sun set, then when they woke up, they realized that the little man was gone. True to his word, it had been the best sex they'd ever had and they'd learned a lot about the art of communication.

Later that evening, the little man, all dressed in green, arrived at his house in suburbia. Entering the kitchen, he tossed his green top hat on the counter, grabbed his wife, and, hand on her breast, gave her a deep, passionate kiss. "Forget dinner," he said in his natural voice, having to clear his throat several times after an hour of squeaking. "It all starts with kissing."

"Damn, Bernie," his wife said, lifting her five-foot-tall husband so she could press her mound against his hard cock. "You've been doing the leprechaun thing again, haven't you?"

His wide grin was her answer.

"I love it when you come home all hot like this," she said, a wide smile on her face. "You're such a con artist, but I do like the results." She turned off the stove and they rushed into the bedroom.

Epilogue

THE FOLLOWING YEAR, MISSY AND PETE WROTE A BOOK titled *Leprechaun Loving: Communication Advice from a Magical Being*. It sold several hundred thousand copies and was translated into fourteen different languages.

Creating a Bestseller

※

The book is just great, the story's tight and well written, but it lacks the erotic scenes that might make it a bestseller.

The letter had gone on to detail several places in the manuscript where her agent thought that a sizzling lovemaking session would add to the text.

Mandy sighed. She had to admit that she agreed with Norman. When she'd written the sections he referred to, she'd realized that a good erotic encounter would add immeasurably to the effect, but she had found herself unable to write one. She'd created a sort of fade-to-black and moved on to the "morning after."

Putting the letter to one side on her desk, she booted up

her computer and brought up one of the sections in question. Rereading, she knew she had to add something really hot. The characters were begging for it and readers would feel let down if they didn't "do it."

She opened a new document, and after staring at her blank screen for several minutes, she pushed her wheeled desk chair away from her computer and leaned back. Why was she unable to write the needed lovemaking scenes? Obvious. What the hell did she know about hot, kinky sex, especially between people who were little more than strangers at that point in the story?

She wasn't totally without a sexual past, of course. She was over thirty and she'd had boyfriends. Two had been live-ins, if only for a few months each. But the sex with each had been traditional, missionary position. Even her fantasies were pretty plain vanilla.

She went onto the Web, searched for erotic stories, and found plenty. She considered rewriting one or two of those, adapting them to the situation in her manuscript, but the tales all seemed so phony. She wanted to be able to write warm, loving sex between people who cared about each other, even if they weren't in a relationship—not just folks getting it on to scratch an itch.

She had to admit that, in her book, the people who would be involved in the scene didn't know much about each other. The first two encounters were actually little more than one-night stands. Could people have meaningful sex without any kind of relationship?

She sighed. Okay, in the twenty-first century people did that sort of thing. She knew that. She just couldn't write about it, couldn't *feel* it. And if she couldn't feel it, she couldn't commit it to paper—or to her word processor.

"It's not that difficult," a male voice said from behind her.

She whirled around and saw a man standing by the door, leaning casually against the jamb. He was sexy as hell, with shoulder-length deep brown hair caught at the nape of his neck with a black cord and a Kirk Douglas cleft in his chin. He was tall and lean; his body well displayed in a tight black shirt, skintight black jeans, and cowboy boots. And he had the most brooding bedroom eyes above a devilish, wrong-side-of-the-tracks grin. He looked like a bad-boy hero from one of the romance novels she enjoyed reading so much.

She stared, unable to say a word, committing him to memory. *Next time I need a magnetic, erotic, totally sexy guy for one of my books, he's it.* She placed a hand over her pounding heart and tried to calm her racing pulse. She wasn't afraid, however, even though a strange man was standing in her office in her condo. She felt that he belonged.

Finally able to breathe, she said, "Who are you?"

"I have no idea," he said, "but you can call me . . ." He seemed puzzled and tilted his head to one side. "Jared. That sounds like a good name."

Jared was the name of the hero of her current novel. "Okay, Jared. What the hell are you doing here?"

"I'm here for you," he said, his smile revealing white, even teeth in the middle of his deeply tanned face.

Here for me? A strangler? A rapist? But as quickly as those thoughts flitted through her brain, she dismissed them. She didn't know why, but she felt no malice from him and had no fear. "Here for me? What the hell does that mean?"

"Again, I have no idea. I just know that I was summoned in some way, so here I am. What did you do to summon me?"

"I didn't summon you in any way."

"Don't be silly. Of course you did. Think. What were you doing when I showed up?"

The book. The sex scenes. She was thinking . . . She couldn't go any further. "I don't know."

"Oh, Mandy, stop fooling yourself. You certainly do know, and now that you do, I do, too. You've written a book. A good book. But it's missing hot sex. I would bet that's what I'm here for, and it's what I do best. I'm really good at hot, wicked sex." Again that charming, enticing grin, this time accompanied by a slow, sexy wink.

"Arrogant, too," she said, glaring at him. She wasn't going to have sex with him just so she could create spicy scenes for her novel.

"True, but I was only telling you the truth. And yes, you're going to have sex with me just so you can improve your book."

"Dream on." She tried for mad, suppressing the urge to smile at him. He was almost irresistible.

"Not me, you. I'm your dream. And your reality."

"Nonsense."

"Do you have any better explanation? I'm here because you wanted me here." He looked down. "No one really looks like this." He walked over to a full-length mirror that hung on the door of the closet in the bedroom she'd turned into her office. "I look like the cover of a romance novel. I can't be real. If I were a woman, I'd turn me on. Admit it. I'm a hunk."

"Okay. You're sexy as hell. But so what?"

"Sexy as hell. How sexy *is* hell?" There was a chuckle in his voice, then he lowered it until it flowed like honey. "Hmm. Sexy enough to have your nipples all tight and your pussy twitching and wet?"

He was right, but . . . "Now cut that out and leave me alone."

He moved behind her, lifted her short hair from the back of her neck, and kissed her there. Then his tongue swirled, making a small wet pattern above the back of her T-shirt. His mouth slid to the tendon that extended from her neck to her shoulder and he bit her.

She felt a flush fill her, further swelling the flesh in her groin. "Cut that out!"

"You don't really want that, now do you? I'm here for your pleasure, so accept it. Accept me."

He placed one hand on each shoulder and turned her swivel chair until she faced him. "You want this, and you know you do. Stop lying about it."

She was speechless. He was right and she knew it. She did want to go along with everything he had in mind. He was only a figment of her imagination, after all, so what was the harm? Nothing could really happen.

"Good." He crouched between her knees and looked up to her. She could smell his spicy cologne in the heat that radiated from his body. "From what I read in your mind, and in that letter, of course," he said, tapping the note from her agent, "you need two things. You need a good fuck, and you need to be able to write about it. I can help with both, and I will."

He was almost hypnotic. Her pulse sped and her hands trembled, this time not from surprise but from arousal. He grinned, then reached out and whipped her shirt off over her head. "Okay. Now, about the writing . . ." He tweaked one nipple through the fabric of her cotton bra. "In the book, women should never wear cotton undies. Silk, lace, satin. Black or red. Maybe palest blue if they want to appear untouched." He pulled her forward and unhooked her bra and she let him, unable to resist.

"Mmm," he purred. "Nice dark nipples against very white flesh. I like that. Actually, that's a good phrase. 'Dark nipples against white flesh.' Remember it for your writing."

He touched the point of her chin with the tips of his

fingers and pulled her face toward him. "Kissing. Very important. Tongue stabbing into your mouth. Teeth nipping at your lower lip." He demonstrated and heat stabbed through her. After several long minutes, he settled back on his haunches. "Swollen lips afterward from hot, hard kissing. Driving her wild. More good phrases."

His slightly clinical talk and his actions were driving her crazy. He was a stranger yet she wanted him. Apparently hungry, erotic sex between people who hardly knew one another was possible.

"His mouth reached for her erect nubbins." His tongue lapped at her flesh as his fingers swirled over her. "His teeth scraped." He nibbled at her nipples, drew first one, then the other into his mouth. Her hips wanted to move so much that she could barely sit still. While his mouth sucked at one nipple, his fingers pinched and pulled at the other.

He settled back. "Flushed skin. Breathing ragged. Using the flat of his tongue to lave her flesh." He grinned. "You getting all this? No? Probably not, heat of passion and all that. Okay, I'll see to it that there's a list of good words, phrases, and ideas on your computer later. For now, just feel."

He picked her up, Rhett Butler–style, and carried her into her bedroom, then stood her beside her bed. Her knees would hardly hold her, so he supported her with one arm and used the other hand to unfasten her jeans and pull them off along with her socks and panties. He dropped everything on the floor. "You exude the scent of sex," he said, "and you're so hot now you feel like you're going to explode. Not yet, Mandy. You've got a lot more to learn."

He was right. She burned for him.

He lifted her onto the bed. "You will be frantic for release before this day is over," he said. "For now, feel the hunger spiral through you."

She shuddered, knowing she was eager to experience everything he could give her. Imagination? Not very likely. This was altogether too real.

He spread her legs and crawled between. "Pussies are so beautiful," he said, "lips all swollen, skin slick with juices." He parted her with his thumbs. "You're deep pink with arousal, sizzling with need."

He licked the length of her slit with the flat of his tongue. "You taste salty and my tongue slides over you so easily." He tightened the tip of his tongue and thrust it into her opening. He pushed, then released, pushed, then released until she was wild, the pressure building low in her belly.

Then he lapped at her clit, tongue swirling around it, then flicking the tip. She arched her back and her hips thrashed. Her breath caught in her lungs until she thought she'd expire. The storm built.

When he sucked her swollen clit and bit lightly, her climax finally crashed over her and she heard her own keening wail of pleasure. She couldn't control her body, but despite her thrashing, he managed to keep his mouth fastened on her, sucking, drawing the last bit of pleasure from her.

Eventually he rested his head on her belly as she slept. When she awoke from her doze she was briefly afraid he'd be gone, but she felt the weight of his head on her shoulder, arm across her ribs. "Mmm," she purred.

"That was a good start," he said, his voice like lava flowing through her. "And there's so much more I can show you. I'll teach you how to use your mouth on me, along with all the accompanying hot words. We'll do rear entry, anal sex, maybe even spend a little time with a whip or a paddle." She was a little doubtful about that last stuff. However . . . "And all the words will be in your head and in a document called 'Sizzlers' on your computer."

She knew she could write some things now, but who cared. Doing it for real was much more fun than writing about it.

Creating a Bestseller:
The Next Chapter

❧

ᴊᴀʀᴇᴅ ʜᴀᴅ ᴅɪsᴀᴘᴘᴇᴀʀᴇᴅ ʟᴀᴛᴇ ᴛʜᴇ ᴘʀᴇᴠɪᴏᴜs ᴇᴠᴇɴɪɴɢ, but he reappeared that afternoon. When Mandy saw him, she yelled, "He loved the scene I wrote."

"Who loved it?"

"My agent. Norman. I emailed him several rewritten pages and he was ecstatic. He called me a little while ago. 'A few more scenes like this and the book's a shoo-in,' he said." Mandy jumped up and threw her arms around Jared's neck.

"Did you create a scene based on what we did yesterday?"

"I did," Mandy said, suddenly embarrassed. Jared had arrived the previous day to help her with the erotic sections of her book, and as a result, they'd had the most explosive sex Mandy had ever had.

"Don't chicken out," Jared said, his voice still sensual and compelling. "I assume you haven't got any ideas for the next one."

"I can do it," she said. "I looked over the document you created on my computer, and there are a lot of words and phrases I can use." How he'd created that file, or even who or what he was, remained a mystery.

Still awake sometime around three a.m., she'd decided that he was a figment of her imagination. The entire Jared thing had happened only in her mind. But when her curiosity had gotten the better of her and she'd booted up her computer, sure enough, the file called "Sizzlers" was there, right where he'd said it would be. She'd read it, written a scene involving her characters at a feverish pace, then back in bed, lapsed into dreamless slumber.

Imagination. Not!

Now Jared was here, in her office once more, looking just as sexy as he had the previous evening. She hadn't dreamed or imagined him. Had she?

"No, you didn't imagine me," he said, "but that's not really the point. You say you can write another scene on your own. Have you tried?"

She hesitated a bit too long. "I would guess that you have and it didn't work."

She let out a long sigh. "Well, I have the words, but I can't get into her feelings."

"I don't wonder. Just yesterday you thought that two

people who weren't in a long-term relationship couldn't have meaningful, enjoyable sex. I think you've gotten over that part. We had the equivalent of a one-night stand and it was explosive. Right?" He hooked his thumbs in the front pockets of his jeans and leaned his hip against her desk.

"I have to admit that you were right about that," she said. "You cared about my pleasure and, to be honest, I cared about you, too, even though I hardly know you. I guess that was enough, and it was enough for the characters in my book."

"Good. Step one. But now you need a few more activities. You need to know how it feels to be fucked in the ass, and what it's like to share the joy of toys. Hey, that's a good phrase. The joy of toys. I'll write that down."

Mandy couldn't reply. She was totally incapable of talking about kinky stuff the way Jared did, although she'd have to, at least for the book.

"Okay, let's create a scene. Tell me about the one you need to write."

Mandy swallowed hard and twisted her fingers in her lap. "Well," she said softly, "my couple is in the backyard of a friend's house. There's a pool and, well . . ."

Jared waved his hand and they were there. The house was swathed in fog, but the backyard was relatively clear. Sunlight streamed through the branches of several large trees. Gardens were a riot of color with spring and fall flowers, all blooming simultaneously. The pool was tremendous, with mist hanging over it. A blanket was spread on the carefully manicured grass, and a champagne bucket, filled with ice and an open bottle, lay beside two tulip glasses.

"How did you do that?" Mandy asked, shocked to her toes.

"I have no idea," Jared said, wiggling his bare toes in the grass.

Then she sighed. "It's lovely."

"I hope you like it." He removed his shirt. "So, you know that you need more descriptive words for the male body. I thought I'd help." He pulled off his jeans and stood in the middle of the blanket wearing only his briefs. "Okay, I don't mean to be egotistical, but I am built as you wanted me to be." He ran his palms down his sides. "Washboard abs, wide shoulders, narrow hips. I've got well-developed thighs and even great feet." He wiggled his toes again then winked at her. "I hope you like looking at me."

She certainly did. She wasn't a stranger to male bodies, but his exuded sex, causing a flush to spread over her body. She felt fluids begin to leak from her . . .

"Cunt," Jared said. "Fluids leak from your cunt." He laughed. "You have to learn to think those words, too, so you can write them. *Cunt. Pussy. Snatch.* Like that."

"I know those words."

"Right," he said, unbelieving. "So say them. Say cunt."

She had to clear her throat. "Okay, cunt."

"Good girl. Now add pussy and snatch."

After a long exhalation, she added, "Pussy and snatch," almost stuttering.

He reached out and squeezed her shoulders while placing a light kiss on her lips. "You're wonderful." He stepped back. "Now for the male body. You need cock, dick, rod—member, if you must."

"I know those words, too, and I've even written a few, but it's just hard to say them."

"Hard. That's a great word. And really true." He pulled down his shorts and wiggled his hips. "Raging hard-on, rigid staff. You've read all the words and now you know what they mean."

She gazed at him. Sure, he lacked humility, but he was certainly right about the hard part. He was magnificent. "You're playing with me," she said, smiling.

"Right you are. Lighten up, Mandy. Relax."

She tried, but with Jared standing on a red plaid blanket in a yard in the middle of nowhere, it was difficult. She just stared.

"I love the way you look at me," he said. "How about, moves like a feral creature, sleek, a stalking panther."

"God, yes," she said, almost drooling. She couldn't decide whether he was narcissistic or charming or both, but he certainly turned her on. She stared at his erection.

"Say something," he said, lightly stroking himself.

She coughed. "Okay. Rigid rod."

"Better. Describe what you see."

In for a penny . . . "Your cock is beautiful, hard, and long. There's fluid leaking from the head, and you look like you're ready for action."

"Great. And I am. You turn me on, you know."

She hadn't thought of that. She was partly responsible for that wonderful part of him. She couldn't suppress her grin. "And you turn me on," she said.

He approached her and slowly unbuttoned her blouse and removed it and her bra, kissing and licking each part as it was revealed. "So beautiful," he purred, and she felt beautiful. He knelt at her feet and undressed the rest of her. Standing, he said, "Touch me. Get to know what a hard cock feels like. The phrase 'velvet over steel' is cliché but it describes a hard-on as well as any other." He held her hands and placed her palms against his erection. "I hope that feels as good to you as it does to me." Still holding her hands against him, he slowly moved his hips, thrusting between her fingers.

He suddenly pulled away. "Not yet. Let's take a swim."

"Swim?" she said, wanting him to make love to her again.

"Water's so much fun to play in." He grabbed her wrist. "Last one in . . ."

Together they jumped into the deep end of the pool, played, and splashed for a few minutes. Then he turned her so that her chest and belly were against the cold tiles, his warm, hard flesh against her back. She was effectively pinned to the side of the pool. She felt his rigid member probing between her cheeks. He lifted her slightly so she had to hold on to the edge, grabbed her hips, and entered her pussy from behind. "I love filling you, sliding into your slick passage." In slow motion he withdrew, then entered her again. He was driving her wild with need, each thrust pressing her breasts against the rough concrete edging. She arched her back, giving him a better angle.

"Here's another thrill," he growled into her ear. "Look up."

She gasped. Now there were several other couples in lawn chairs around the pool, watching everything they were doing. "How do you like being watched?"

"It's . . ."

His chuckle was warm in her ear. "Yeah, it is, isn't it? I knew you'd find it as erotic as I do." He thrust into her again and listened to her moan. "Everyone can hear your pleasure."

She was mortified, but it was also incredibly hot. All those eyes, staring at her face, reading every expression, knowing what Jared was doing. Her body jerked and her breasts bounced with each thrust and she couldn't control her gasps of delight.

Jared reached around and rubbed her clit, driving her mad. Then one of the men got up from his lawn chair and moved to the edge of the pool, settling himself so her face was between his legs. His dick was slender, but fully aroused. Tangling his fingers in her hair, he pulled Mandy's head up and gazed into her eyes. When she opened her mouth, he slid his cock inside, gently fucking her hot, moist cavern.

Jared was still buried in her pussy while his talented fingers massaged her clit. She came then, screaming, while the cock pulled out of her mouth and sprayed come on her breasts.

Gasping for air, she suddenly found herself back in her bedroom, spread on her bed. Jared was straddling her waist, cock nestled between her breasts. "This way works, too," he said, his slick member sliding up and down her breastbone. He took her hands and used them to press her breasts together as he fucked her tits. "You have great tits," he said, then threw his head back and roared in complete release. Semen sprayed over her chin and cheeks. He scooped a bit onto one finger and held it to her lips. "Taste, so you can describe that, too."

She did. "Salty, tangy, and sort of slithery."

He laughed again. "There are better words, but I'll leave that up to you." He climbed off the bed, pulled a light blanket over her, and slowly faded away.

Mandy slept well.

Later that evening she wrote another scene for the book and sent it off to her agent. She wanted his reaction, but she really didn't need it. She knew it was good.

She glanced at her watch. It was only seven thirty and she realized that she was starving. She backed up her files, put her computer to sleep, and wondered whether she'd ever see Jared again. She didn't need him anymore, not for her writing anyway, but she'd be empty without his lovemaking.

Depressed at the thought of not seeing him again, she

decided to treat herself to a bowl of wonton soup and some chicken with cashews from Cantonese Empire on the corner. As she stood outside her apartment waiting for the elevator, a man walked out of the apartment next to hers and joined her at the elevator. "Hi," he said. "I just moved in."

"Hello," she said, extending her hand, "nice to meet you. I'm Mandy."

He wasn't particularly good-looking, but he had a sparkle in his eyes and a slightly knowing smile. "Glad to meet you, too, Mandy." He extended his hand. "My name's Jared."

Nah, she thought. *Coincidence! However . . .*

Thongs

❧

EVER WORN A PAIR OF THONG PANTIES? I HAVE, AND WEAR-
ing them has changed my life. Okay, not my entire life, but
my attitude toward lots of things, including my husband and
our sex life.

It all began a few weeks ago. I took several pairs of my
panties out of the washer and the elastic was shredded. Little
strings were tangled around half the stuff I'd laundered and
the waistbands were a wreck. It was time for some new stuff.
I could have gone to Walmart, but I'd just gotten a small
bonus at work, so I decided to treat myself. Victoria's Secret,
here I come.

During my lunch hour the next day, I drove over to the
mall. I gazed in the lingerie shop's window, then entered

and walked over to look at the panties. They had dozens of styles: bikinis, briefs, sporty cotton athletic-looking ones, things called cheekies, and hip huggers. They had panties in every color, shape, and size: fancy cotton, lace, silk, satin, ruffles, bows, ribbons, flowers—you get the idea. They had just about every design you could imagine. And, of course, they had thongs.

I wandered over to the display and I guess I made a face. They looked truly uncomfortable and like they were made for teenyboppers, so I walked away. "They really aren't difficult to get used to, and they're very sexy. You've got just the right shape for them." The salesgirl looked to be about my age, late twenties, and had a nice but not anorexic figure. "You should really try a pair."

I glanced at the fitting room, but she quickly said, "I'm sorry, but you can't try them on, I'm afraid. Not allowed. But you should really take a pair for a test drive."

"Nah," I said. She was just trying to make a sale. "I think I'll find something else."

"I thought just like you before I tried a pair. Let me suggest something." She took a pair from the rack. "These are on sale, soft, stretchy lace, and they'll give you the feel of wearing a thong. I'll bet once you try a pair for a day you'll never wear anything else."

Just the right shape, she'd said. Okay, I've got a pretty nice figure, but I'm certainly not anorexic, and I've got a substantial ass. I was used to having my panties snug against my behind. This little piece of fabric wouldn't cover my cheeks at all.

I glanced at the price tag. Surprised, I said, "They really are on sale."

"I'm not trying to con you into buying something just because. If I were, I'd sell you lingerie for quite a bit more money. Please, do me a favor. I'm sure about this."

She'd convinced me. I had intended to buy several pairs of panties, but I decided that, since she was so convinced I'd like them, I'd take one pair for a test run and make a decision later. "Okay, you've sold me." She showed me ones in my size and I picked a pair in red. Might as well go all the way.

AT HOME, I FOUND A RED DEMI BRA IN THE BACK OF MY underwear drawer, and after my shower the following morning, put it on and slithered into my new thong. The panty was a wide band of lace that stretched around my hips with a strip of matching satin that slipped between my legs. The front just covered my mound and the thong narrowed in the back to slide between my cheeks. I noticed some pubic hair sticking out and used a little pair of scissors to trim my bush. I looked at myself in the mirror and, while I watched, wiggled my hips. It felt funny to feel my ass cheeks jiggle, and as I moved, the strap slipped deeper into my ass crack until it lay tightly against my anus.

Sexy? You bet. I found myself getting wet just feeling the

lace against my crotch. Damn if the saleslady wasn't right. I looked myself over, sizeable breasts filling my bra nicely and those amazingly sexy panties seemed to point directly to my crotch. *Jeff will be delighted,* I thought.

"Holy shit, babe," my husband said when he saw me, eyes almost bugging out of his head. "Those are sexy as hell." Let me assure you that I haven't seen that look on his face since we were first married.

"Sorry, big guy," I teased. "Work calls." With his eyes never leaving my body, I pulled on a pair of tight slacks and a sweater, slipped on knee-high stockings and low-heeled shoes. I decided to put a pair of my old panties in my purse in case the thong got too uncomfortable. Pocketbook in hand, I all but ran out the door. The last thing Jeff saw was my jiggling fanny. Let him think about me all day. I was sure that, with my new undies, I'd be thinking of him.

Actually, I did think of him, but I found myself getting turned on by fantasies of almost every cute guy I saw. I'm sure that a suit-wearing man on the bus checked out my butt under my slacks and grinned at me. The guy who worked in the cubicle next to mine gave me a curious look after I walked down the hall. At lunch, the fellow standing in line behind me in the cafeteria glanced at me, then at my wedding ring, and sighed. Okay, maybe it was all my imagination, but those thoughts kept my nipples hard and my pussy wet all day.

As I walked around, my pussy lips sort of parted and the thong pressed against my clit so that, as the day wore on, I had to change into my old-fashioned cotton panties just to keep the crotch of my slacks from getting soaked. I was going to masturbate in the stall, but I wanted to save it for Jeff. I changed back before leaving work.

My husband had gotten home before me. "I left early," he said, grabbing my ass as I closed our front door behind me. "I kept thinking about that underwear you've got on, and I couldn't wait to get my hands on you."

I've never been the aggressive type, but I turned him so his back was against the door and pressed my mound against the front of his slacks. Oh, yeah, he was right about where his thoughts were. The hard ridge of him was obvious. I reached down and squeezed him. "I get the message."

He kissed me. And I mean *kissed* me. I love the way Jeff kisses when he's hot. His kiss said it all. While his tongue was busy in my mouth, his hands found my breasts. He squeezed my tits, somehow pushing my breasts over the tops of my bra cups so he could pinch my turgid nipples. I was as aroused as he was. I unzipped his fly and found his cock with only a layer of cotton between my fingers and his hardness.

"God, baby," he said. "Let's move this into the bedroom."

I backed off, then wiggled my way down the hall to our room. He stripped out of his clothes really quickly and stretched out on the bed. I remained standing. I was getting into it, enjoying teasing him. "Not so fast," I said. I had no idea where this brazen woman had come from, but from the look in Jeff's eyes, he was loving it all.

"Come on, baby. I'm so hungry for you."

"I know, and I like it." I grabbed the bottom of my sweater and slowly pulled it off over my head. My boobs were still spilling over the top of the bra, and as he watched I unhooked it and slowly took it off. He's always loved my tits so I held them out for him.

When he reached for me, I moved away and said, "Don't get grabby. Put your hands back down." When he looked puzzled, I said, "No hands."

"This isn't like you," he said, curling his fingers as a simulation of squeezing my breasts. "You're never . . ."

"Are you complaining?"

He sighed and smiled. "No, not at all." He put his hands beside his hips on the bed, palms up.

"That's a good boy." I leaned over the bed and let my boobs hang over Jeff's mouth. I slowly lowered one so he could suck on my nipple. He knows just how hard to pull to make me crazy. I felt the tiny panties getting still wetter. I stood and pulled off my slacks. As I started to remove the thong, he said, "Leave that on. It's like gift wrap for my favorite part of you."

His cock was sticking straight up so I straddled him. He pushed the strip of material to one side and, grabbing my hips, rammed me down onto his dick. I was sopping so he slid inside with no trouble. God, he felt so good, filling my pussy with his hard flesh. I wanted, needed, took. I think we were both a little crazed, so I raised and lowered myself on his cock faster and faster. Then, without his erection ever leaving my body, he flipped me over and pounded his cock into me.

His fingers found my clit through the lacy material and the sort of muffled feeling, combined with his hard cock inside of me, drove me over the edge. My scream was followed almost immediately by his. We collapsed together and dozed off. I awoke, thinking about the following day and my trip to Victoria's Secret for more thong panties. Wow!!!

He stood and gazed at what he'd uncovered. Her skin was as lovely as he'd imagined, china white and smooth. Her breasts full and ripe beneath the remaining thin layer of fabric. Through the silk of her pantaloons, he could see the dark triangle at the tops of her thighs. He used his fingers to easily delve beneath the legs of her pantaloons to find the tops of her stockings and slowly, leisurely rolled them down.

When he stroked the arch of her foot, she kicked out at him, catching him lightly on the chest. "That will never do," he said. "You really must not struggle."

She kicked harder, pounding her heels onto the bed. "You'll hurt yourself that way." He rummaged in his closet and found a piece of soft cord, which he cut in half with the knife. Then he efficiently tied each ankle to the footboard of the bed. She was now truly helpless, open for him.

"I'm really sorry I had to do that," he said, not sure whether he was sorry or not.

She sputtered, "I am a lady, and thus I can't think of any words vile enough for you."

"How about bastard?" he said with a laugh. "Son of a bitch usually works as well. Or motherfucker. Shit."

"Oh," she uttered, glaring at him. "You're no gentleman."

His laugh was full and rich. "Right. Got it. You're a lady and I'm a bastard. Good for you. We've got the roles in this little drama sorted out."

Now that she was completely immobilized, he used the

knife to remove the rest of her clothing until she lay, naked and panting, unable to cover herself.

His sigh was deep with longing, but despite the heaviness in his groin, he kept himself in check. "I'll tell you what," he said. "I won't ravish you until you beg me to."

It was her turn to laugh. "That will never happen."

He merely smiled. Then he slid his fingertips over her ankle and calf. "You will, my love. I guarantee it."

He began at her toes, playing with each, sucking one after another until they were curling. "Do you like that?" he asked.

"No," she snapped. "You're merely irritating me." Her tone had become imperious.

He moved to her hands, trapped by the ropes. He swirled his tongue in her palm, then nibbled on each finger. He watched her eyes, seeing them become heavy lidded with the desire to sink into the pleasure he knew he was giving her.

Finally, her breasts tempted him beyond his ability to hold back. He sat on the edge of the bed and laved each without touching the now-erect nipple. He saw her breathing speed up and knew she was slowly succumbing to the erotic joys he was providing. But she wasn't nearly ready to beg yet.

"You want me to suck your nipples as no man has ever done, but you're too proud to admit it."

"I want no such thing!"

He chuckled, licking a path from her breastbone to one darkened areola, but no farther. He teased her for long moments, watching her become more and more aroused. "I know you want it, so I'll give you what you crave, just this once."

He fastened his mouth over one nipple and sucked, while lightly pinching the other. Obviously unable to control her body any longer, her hips bucked and her fingers curled into fists.

Alternating between nipples, he drove her higher. "Tell me you want this," he said, knowing she wasn't ready yet.

"Not a chance," she said, barely able to draw enough breath into her lungs to speak.

"Oh, you will," he said, biting one erect bud, causing her to gasp, not in pain but in pleasure. Her eyes slid closed.

Then he moved between her legs. Her pussy was already swollen, flowing with her juices. Her erect clit protruded slightly from the nest of curls, begging in its own way for his touch and his mouth. Slowly, teasing her with each stroke, he slid his fingers through her wetness. "Your body wants me. Feel how wet it is. You've probably never felt like this before, reaching for something but you don't know what."

"I'm not reaching . . . for anything," she said, her words coming in little bursts.

Then his finger found her clit, tapping lightly on the tip. Her hips bucked, needing, wanting. He swirled around the sides and massaged the length of her slit, then slid one finger inside her just a tiny bit.

"No," she sobbed. "Go away!"

"You don't really mean that."

She wept and he knew that she was slowly coming to terms with her body's needs. He stretched out between her thighs and licked her slit, then sucked her clit. With one finger slightly inside her, he felt the tiny spasms that pre-saged orgasm, and stopped, leaving her body hanging on the precipice.

"Now say please," he growled and heard her answering moan. "All right," he said, slowly building the pleasure again with his mouth and fingers. Again he left her without the final touch he knew she craved, only blowing on the wet skin. "Say please."

Her hips thrashed. "I know what can relieve your hunger, and I can give it to you. There's such pleasure in it for you. Don't deny yourself. Just say please."

Her eyes opened and she stared at him, eyes glazed with want. She took a deep breath and he again blew on her wet skin. "Please," he said, hot breath laving her slit. "Say it."

Head dropping to one side, she said, "Don't make me."

"I will make you say it, love. I want to hear you beg."

She waited a long moment, then said, "Please. Help me."

He quickly removed his clothes and, penis totally erect and hard as steel, knelt between her legs and positioned himself at her opening. Then he rammed into her slick, tight passage, causing her to scream out in pleasure. As he pistoned, he rubbed her clit until he could feel the waves of her orgasm squeeze his cock. The fact that his fantasy had begun with her a virgin and now she accommodated him totally didn't faze him.

"CAPTAIN BLOOD AGAIN?" A FEMALE VOICE SAID.

Larry snapped back to the present, barely noticing the credits at the end of the movie roll on his TV screen. His wife, Anne, now home from her reading group, lay between his legs, mouth ready for him.

"When I finish with you," she said, licking her lips and flicking the tip of her tongue over the dripping head of his cock, "you'll be able to last longer later when you tie me to the bed."

She engulfed his erection with her hot, wet mouth and he came. He had the best, most understanding wife ever, and he was going to fuck her brains out all night.

Movie Mania—
Part 2: The Alien

❦

$\mathcal{L}$ARRY'S WIFE, ANNE, ENJOYED MOVIES AS MUCH AS HE did, but she tended to want to discuss them with him during the film, often commenting on the actors' performances or costumes and guessing at the ending. She was usually also knitting or doing a crossword puzzle at the same time. On the other hand, he preferred total immersion, lights dim, HDTV turned up so he felt completely surrounded by the film.

Larry loved his wife and wouldn't trade her for anything, but on one precious evening a week, while Anne joined several others to critique books, he got to watch movies his way. Usually, either Turner Classic Movies or the Fox Movie

Channel showed something he enjoyed, new or classic. Tonight, he found a *Star Wars* marathon.

He loved sci-fi movies and specifically enjoyed the aliens; aliens could be anyone and do anything, especially with the great special effects that had been added in recent years.

Lying naked, watching between his toes, Larry let Luke, Leia, and Han wash over him, and as usual, he drifted into his own world.

She had appeared in his bedroom, looking sort of like Leia, with braids curled around her ears. Yes, he'd like to slowly unbraid her hair and let it flow over his body. He didn't worry about why or how; he just enjoyed looking at her and feeling his cock react.

"I know you want me," she said, and Lord, did he. "It's the pheromones we aliens exude. We want you to desire us."

He said nothing, just stared, entranced.

"We want to learn everything there is to enjoy about this thing you call 'intercourse.' We have read books and know the facts, but we gather that there is so much more than the *how* of it. We want to experience it, to learn the *why*."

"With me?"

"Why not? Don't you know how to do it?"

He snorted. "Of course I do. I just wondered why you selected me."

"Luck. Actually, I have no idea. Our leader sent many of us out to gather information on all subjects. I'm one of those designated to learn about sex."

"I'll be happy to show you."

"No, just let me do the things I've read about and see what happens."

She walked to the side of the bed, leaned over, and kissed him. "I understand that kissing is a desirable part of the lead-up to intercourse."

They kissed for several minutes, then she kissed his ears and ran her fingers through his hair. "Yes," she said, "very stimulating." She looked at his cock, hardening more each minute. "I read that the penis gets aroused and stiffens. Is that why it's sticking up like that?"

Somehow he loved the clinical discussion of his reactions. "Yes," he said.

"Good. I can watch it and see which of the erogenous areas causes it to react." He closed his eyes as she played with his ears, nose, and eyelids, commenting on which activities seemed to excite him.

Moving down his body, she tweaked one nipple and his cock twitched. "You really do like that. The book I read said that some men like it and others don't." She licked one nipple, her long, slightly prehensile tongue curling around it and tugging gently.

He swallowed hard, trying to control his body. He reasoned that it wouldn't do to go off yet, especially before she'd learned all she wanted to know. "I like that a lot," he said.

She played with his nipples until they were hard and tight. "They get erect like little penises." Her hands moved to his belly and she inserted one finger into his navel. "I don't care for that," he said with a gasp.

"All right, I won't do it." She moved to his cock, touching, stroking, moving it around. "Our species has nothing like this organ. We donate cells that are fertilized by the male's sperm in laboratories. I'm finding this much more enjoyable."

"On your planet there's no sexual fun? No playing?"

"We have sexual fun. We need to be aroused for the donation process, but it happens within ourselves."

Larry sighed. "How sad."

"Oh, not really. We're content."

"Maybe you'll learn not to be so content when you folks go back home, particularly if there are males of your species learning from our women."

"Maybe," she said, cupping his balls with one hand and fondling his cock with the other. "Some men like this," she said, touching his anus, another squeezing his ass cheeks.

Now she had one hand on his cock, one holding his balls, one with a finger slowly entering his anus, and one on his ass cheeks. Four hands, each with seven long, grasping fingers. Shit, this was heaven. "I'd like to watch you climax," she said.

"That can certainly be arranged." He relaxed and let orgasm overtake him, semen erupting from his cock and flowing over her hand.

"Wonderful," she said. "Now we must have intercourse."

"I'm afraid I don't recover so quickly."

"Of course you do," she said, watching his cock greedily. "My pheromones will help."

Sure enough, almost immediately he was hard again.

"I've read that men like doing it doggie style. I'm not quite sure I understand what that means."

Larry took a deep breath. "If you've got your, eh, parts in the same places our women do, then I'll show you."

"We have created such parts to allow us to experience everything."

Larry guided her onto her hands, all of them, and knees on the bed, and he knelt behind her. Her pussy looked just like a human's, and she was very wet. He rubbed his erection over her flesh, then slowly inserted it into her cunt. "Oh," she said when he was fully inside.

Larry felt a sensation he'd never experienced before. Her vagina, or what they'd created to be a vagina, squeezed him, rhythmically stroking, muscles rippling the length of him. Holding her hips tightly against him, he quickly came inside her, thrusting, bucking, yelling.

He collapsed onto the bed and she was gone.

His fantasy dissolved and he was back in his bedroom, *Star Wars* still playing. "I'm home," Anne called as the front door slammed.

Although Larry had climaxed in his fantasy, in reality he

had saved himself for his wife. She walked into the bedroom and glanced at the TV. She was deliciously aware of what he did while she was out and loved the hot and varied sex that always resulted. "Hmm," she said, "aliens."

"Aliens," he said. "Get naked and I'll tell you *all* about it."

Movie Mania—
Part 3: <u>*ER*</u>

❧

LARRY CLICKED ON THE GUIDE ON HIS TV AND CHECKED both Turner Classic Movies and the Fox Movie Channel. Both films this evening were ones he'd seen quite recently. He sighed. He couldn't stand the commercials on American Movie Classics. Once a week Anne went to the library to meet with her book group, and tonight, while she was gone, he was restless. He'd stretched out on his bed, naked, prepared to watch a good old movie and let his mind wander. Nothing on. He'd have to resort to a weekly program, but only a handful of them were any good.

Okay, he thought, flipping to the guide, *what's on?* One channel was showing *ER* reruns. He'd enjoyed that show while it was on and, although he was pretty sure he'd seen every episode, he clicked over to the right channel just as the show began.

He didn't watch for long. Instead, he closed his eyes and slipped into one of his favorite fantasies. He was in a doctor's office, all white and sterile-looking, with cabinets filled with mysterious doctor stuff and countertops covered with swabs, vials, jars of cotton balls, and boxes of latex gloves. The room smelled of alcohol and disinfectant. He was only wearing one of those light cotton gowns that opened down the back, and he was perched on an examining table covered with white paper that rustled when he shifted position.

He was nervous, as he always was when he went for a checkup. What if he got an erection? The doctor would know and he'd be terribly embarrassed.

The doctor arrived, and as always in his dreams, she was gorgeous. Long red hair hung down her back, surrounding a classically beautiful face. Her body was lush, voluptuous, and desirable. She was wearing a low-cut light blue tank top and short black skirt beneath her white lab coat. Her brief smile was almost wicked, but it disappeared quickly. "Good afternoon, Mr. Thomas," she said. "It's time for your exam. I don't want you to be nervous."

Larry's cock hardened as he watched her take a pair of latex gloves from a box on the counter. He would swear that she put them on purposefully slowly and provocatively, inserting each finger into its place and snapping the wrist. It was as if she knew how hot she was making him. He tried to control his raging hard-on but his usual mental gymnastics were of little help.

She walked around the table and wrapped the blood pressure cuff around his upper arm and pumped it up. With each compression of the little bulb, she exhaled slowly, her hot breath bathing his neck. Finally she released the pressure. "Very good, Mr. Thomas. Your blood pressure is fine."

Sure it was. He was ready to explode and she was telling him his blood pressure was fine. Fat chance.

Over the next few minutes the doctor used an instrument to look in his ears and another to peer down his throat. Then she pushed him onto his back. He looked along the length of his body and saw the large tent that had formed over his erection. Oh well, he could do nothing about it, and surely she'd seen erections before. He took a long, slow breath.

"I'm going to check your heart," she said, attaching the leads of the electrocardiograph machine to his hairy chest. "Now just relax."

He watched the familiar spiking patterns of his heartbeat move across the screen. "Very good," she said. "Let's test a few reactions to see how your heart is doing." She slipped off her lab coat and pulled down the front of her tank, allowing her unfettered breasts to spill free. God, she was fabulous. Great, creamy white breasts with large, deep brown nipples. Her buds were fully erect, and as he stared at them, his cock jerked.

"Interesting," she said, peering at the EKG screen. "I can

watch your heartbeat react to sexual stimuli. Fascinating. This will add to the statistics for my thesis."

Lying on his back in his bedroom, Larry's cock was fully erect and his entire body trembled. The doctor divided her attention between him and the EKG screen. "Let's see what this does." She leaned over so that her breasts hung close to his mouth. "Do you want to suck them?" she asked as the EKG went crazy.

"God, yes," he said.

"Not yet," she replied, straightening. "I don't have all of my data yet." She lifted his exam gown and exposed his cock. "Mmm, nice," she said and Larry felt the blood rushing to his dick. She grabbed it and squeezed, testing his hardness. She pulled it away and let it spring back into place, then glanced again at the screen. "Very nice." She left the table and made a few notes on a pad on the counter. She got a tape measure from one of the cabinets and carefully checked the length and girth of his member. "Interesting," she said sounding totally clinical. "Superior size." Again she wrote on the paper.

Larry felt sweat prickle at his armpits as her cool fingers played with his foreskin. "I like to compare circumcised and uncircumcised penises." He thought he'd spurt right then, but she checked the machine and stopped just before he came.

"It's interesting what I can learn from my EKG. I know exactly what arouses you, and how far I can go without making you come. Fascinating." She made a few more notes, then said, "Turn over."

He did as he was told, making a special effort to position his prick so he was as comfortable as possible. On his bed in the bedroom he turned over as well.

"Now," the doctor said, "let's test a few more reactions." She parted his exam gown, exposing his ass. "Have you ever had anal sex?" When he hesitated, she said, "This EKG acts like a lie detector, so don't fib to me. Have you?"

He cleared his throat. "No," he said, honestly.

"Good. This will be an excellent test." He heard a squishy sound, then felt her lubricate his anus. "Just relax. It will be interesting to see whether this arouses you further." He felt her rub slippery stuff around the rim of his asshole then slowly insert her finger. Slowly, so slowly, filling his ass. "Oh my," she said, "you should see how your entire body reacts to this. It's so interesting."

ANNE ARRIVED HOME FROM HER BOOK GROUP AND SILENTLY tiptoed into the bedroom. She knew that her husband loved his fantasy evenings, and she frequently helped him climax. She saw only his backside and heard his heavy breathing. His fists were clenching and unclenching, trying not to touch himself, waiting to climax until she got home.

She glanced at the TV screen to see what was playing that had triggered this fantasy. *Hmm*, she thought. *Medical stuff.*

He moaned. They'd occasionally talked about fantasies, and she was pretty sure what was driving him crazy. She smiled, slipped into the kitchen, found and washed what she wanted, then stripped off her clothes. She loved playing out fantasies with Larry, and the sex that resulted was always fantastic.

Back in the bedroom she found a bottle of lubricant and covered the end of the long, slender candle she'd brought and gently sat on the edge of the bed. "Don't move," she said, parting his ass cheeks. "This will only take a moment."

He moved his hips, rubbing his erection on the sheet. "Is this really necessary?" he asked through gritted teeth.

"Of course," she said. "It's all part of the exam." She inserted the end of the candle into him and gradually pressed it deeper inside. "Now if you have to come, it's to be expected, and all part of the medical procedure."

"Oh, God," he groaned. "Oh, God." She gently thrust the candle in and out of his anus, watching his hips buck. "Oh, God!" She felt the candle jerk as he came, screaming his satisfaction.

Eventually she pulled the candle out and set it aside. She climbed up beside Larry's body and he wrapped his arm around her. He purred as he nibbled her neck. "That was amazing," he said, finally able to catch his breath. "How did you know?"

"Oh, I'm pretty in tune with you. I guess it was good for you?"

"Babe, it was fantastic. But we'll have to change the sheets."

Anne cupped one of his hands over her breast. "Not just yet," she said. "I've got a few ideas about what you could do for me."

She could feel his soft chuckle. "I've got a few ideas for the doctor, too."

Electric Pencil

❧

$\mathcal{I}$ HAD AN OLD COMPUTER AND AN EVEN OLDER WORD PRO-cessing program. It's called Electric Pencil and, although there are plenty of newer ones with more features, I'm used to this one, and I don't need more than it can do. Like spell-check. Don't need it, don't want it. I write erotic romance novels, and I've had several published. While I'm thinking, I can't deal with having my words flashing on the computer screen with those little underlines reminding me how bad my spelling is. I fix spelling and such after I'm done being creative.

The trouble, if you can call it that, began when the computer died. I tried to get an updated version of Electric Pencil for the spiffy new PC I bought, but it had long since disappeared from the market, replaced by Microsoft Word. After hours of searching, I finally found my original CD-ROM in the back of a file drawer and inserted it into my new machine. The installer started up and an odd question popped open on my screen.

Are you ready for the consequences? Y/N

I didn't remember such a silly question when I first loaded the program on my old computer, but that was a long time ago so maybe I'd forgotten. I typed *Y*.

Are you sure? Y/N

What the hell was this all about? I almost abandoned Electric Pencil and vowed to get used to Microsoft Word, but—what the hell.

Shaking my head, again I typed *Y*.

The machine chugged for several minutes then let out what I swear sounded like a sigh. After the software loaded, I ran the program and opened a new document. It seemed to be working fine.

I typed, "The quick brown fox jumps over the lazy dog." I heard what I thought was my neighbor's dog bark outside, but I ignored it.

"It was a dark and stormy night." There was a sudden flash of lightning and a clap of thunder. Strange. The sun was shining and the sky was a brilliant azure. I'd heard of lightning from a clear blue sky, but I'd never actually experienced it.

I shrugged. Whatever.

But . . . The odd weather combined with the dog barking got me thinking. Okay, magic or voodoo wasn't the first thing that would jump into most people's minds, but remember, I write fiction with unusual activities and situations. I'd been expecting a small royalty check for a short story I'd had published in a magazine, so I typed, "Along with the supermarket ads and magazines, the mailman put the royalty check in my mailbox."

Silly, I know, but I typed it and pressed the Print button. I pulled the paper out of the printer and carried it down in the elevator with me. Using my tiny key, I opened the mailbox. I flipped through the stack of letters and, sure enough, the check was there. Hmm. Upstairs again, I typed, "The bank sent me a letter saying there had been an error in my statement and they were crediting an additional two hundred fifty dollars to my account."

You guessed it. When I riffled through the rest of the envelopes, there was such a letter. Hot damn.

I wondered whether there was a limit to what the program could do and I wanted to give it some thought. I carefully shut the computer down and wandered into my bedroom.

It seemed I could type something and it would come

true. This certainly hadn't been so with my old computer. I wondered how many "wishes" I would get. I didn't want to waste any, so I had to think about the order. If it was going to crap out at some point, I wanted to get my goodies first.

Okay, Kevin, I said to myself. *Concentrate.* I could ask for millions. But I was comfortable enough financially. Having a million wouldn't hurt, of course, but that wasn't at the top of my list.

Health? Sure, but I was healthy and many of my great-grandparents were in their nineties and still going strong.

Stop it, Kevin. You're fooling yourself. Health, wealth, all that was fine, but I knew what I really wanted. Women. Sexy, well-built girls who wanted to make love to me. Fucking. Orgasms. Lots of them. Standing, sitting, outdoors, in the backseat of a car, on a merry-go-round. As you can see, writing has given me a very vivid imagination.

At twenty-five, although I'm far from a virgin, I'm not as experienced as one might think. I write erotica, of course. Good, hot, sweaty, Regency-period romance novels, and my books sell pretty well, if I do say so myself. I know, you probably thought they were all written by women, but although I write as Angela Montaigne, I can assure you that I'm a real guy. I'm not rich, of course, but it's a good adjunct to my day job as an accountant.

People like my books because they are good stories about nice people, filled with lots of kinky sex. And I do mean lots of kinky, really kinky, sex. Unfortunately, I make most of it up. I've never experienced a good part of the stuff I write about.

That's what I wanted most. Lots of women and lots of sex.

I got little sleep that night, considering precisely what and how I should ask.

Another wish would be a great, body-builder physique. In reality I'm pretty average, with a bit of a potbelly. What about my cock? I'd love to be hung like a porn star, but I didn't want to go too far. How should I phrase my sentence so I'd get the most out of it?

The following morning, I brewed myself a pot of strong coffee, booted up my computer, and opened Electric Pencil.

"I've got a pretty great body, and women are attracted to me. Lots of women. They believe that everything I've written about comes from my experiences, and they want to have that kind of sex with me."

Nothing happened. I looked down and my body was still my body. *Shit*. I printed my sentence, hoping that would be the trigger, but still, nothing changed.

Oh well, I thought, *it was a nice dream while it lasted*. I looked at my watch and realized that I had only a few minutes to shave, shower, and dress for work.

I arrived at my office only about five minutes late. "Good morning, Kevin," Shari, the receptionist, said, her voice low and sexy.

"Good morning."

"Doing anything after work? It's Friday, so I thought we could go to a little spot I know about for drinks, then go up to your place."

I almost skidded to a stop in the reception area. Shari was new and all the guys, including yours truly, had been trying to date her, with frosty results. Now she was coming on to me. She was, well, there's no better word than *stacked*. A real hottie, with blond curls and great tits. I can assure you that I wasn't about to look a gift horse in the mouth.

"Sure," I said and she smiled broadly. "We can decide on a time later."

"Great."

When my secretary, Iris, saw me, she asked, "Hey, Kev, how about getting together with me sometime this weekend?" Iris isn't particularly pretty, but she has a body that won't quit.

Holy shit. I thought about my word processor as she motioned to me. She leaned over her keyboard, giving me a great view down her V-neck sweater. She put her mouth close enough to my ear that I could feel her warm breath. "I just finished reading *Marjorie's Memoirs*. Remember page 148? I'd love to try that with you." She wrote her address on a piece of paper and said, "Come around seven."

Page 148? I'd have to look that up, but I'd love to try anything from any of my books. Particularly with Iris. *Come around seven.* Sounded good to me. Especially the *come* part.

Things were pretty quiet for the remainder of the day, but Shari was standing beside the office door as I was leaving just after five. "I've been waiting for you." She laced her fingers through mine and almost dragged me into the elevator. Several of the guys winked at me and, stepping back, left the elevator empty.

She was all over me, hands everywhere. As we passed the third floor on the way down, she grabbed my crotch. "Oooh," she purred. "You're really big. I love a well-built man."

I pried her from me as we reached the main floor and together we exited the building. "I'd love to skip the drinks and go straight to your place. You live near here, right?"

"Just a short subway ride away," I said, panting, almost unable to function.

People stared at us on the subway. Couples necking on the train isn't unusual, but Shari was uncontrollable. Several guys chuckled and nodded at my luck.

At one point, she reached around my waist and cupped my ass cheeks, pressing her pubic bone against my huge boner. It was all I could do not to come in my slacks.

Once inside my apartment, Shari stripped off her clothes and began to undress me. Let me tell you, she was more voluptuous naked than I could have dreamed. Big breasts with pale brown nipples, already tight and pointed, a tiny waist, and long legs. She was obviously not a real blond because her thick pubic hair was dark brown.

She got me naked quickly and all but dragged me into the bedroom. "God, you are so gorgeous," she purred. "I never realized."

She pushed me down onto the bed and, taking only a moment to cover my cock with a condom she'd brought with her, she mounted me, sliding her soaked pussy onto my shaft with no preamble. "So big," she moaned, levering herself up and down on me. "I can't get enough of you."

Her tits bounced with the rhythm of my mostly unnecessary thrusts. She did all the work until I came. It would have been impossible not to, with Shari's great tits and tight pussy.

She reached between us and rubbed herself until she screamed, orgasmed, and collapsed on top of me. She was soon ready to go again and, with a little hand job, I was, too. This time I turned her onto her back and drove into her. Then I moved her legs so her ankles were over my shoulders and pounded, coming again quickly.

With little conversation, we had a burger at a small spot around the corner, then came back to my place and fucked again. Finally, exhausted, she left to find a cab home.

I was in heaven. I'd had more sex that evening than I'd had in the last month. I slept well.

The next day was Saturday and I usually turned out twenty or thirty pages. Today I was brain-locked, unable to think about anything except Shari and Iris. Electric Pencil must be responsible.

I had a little shopping to do, so I went to my neighborhood

supermarket. Quite a few women approached me, and three gave me their phone numbers. Two had long, loud arguments with the guys they were with. The checkout girl almost fell over herself and wrote her address on the back of my credit card slip.

I made a few more stops: the dry cleaner, the pharmacy for condoms, and the liquor store for a bottle of wine to take to Iris's, but I made sure I was waited on by men. I couldn't deal with any more panting females.

I showed up at Iris's apartment at precisely seven. I'd looked up page 148, a scene about sex in the shower. Wine in one hand, I used the other to ring her doorbell.

Iris answered the door dressed in a lacy, see-through peignoir with nothing beneath. "Hi, Iris," I said, handing her the wine and trying not to gape.

She made quick work of opening the bottle and pouring two glasses. "Let's drink them in the bathroom. I've got a great stall shower, just like in the book. And it's got a French shower head."

She all but dragged me to the back of the apartment and turned on the water. I took a quick drink, then stripped off my clothes. Needless to say I was already hard as a rock.

"Got protection?" she asked.

I reached into my pants pocket and pulled out a condom.

She huffed out a little breath, opened the medicine cabinet, and dropped several more onto the floor where they would be handy. She obviously had quite an opinion of me.

Sliding her peignoir to the floor, she stepped beneath the spray and pulled me in behind her. She poured body wash onto a scrubby and lathered herself, paying particular attention to her breasts. They were of average size, but with smoky nipples that quickly became erect. Then she switched to my body, rubbing me all over with the slightly scratchy fabric.

She bent over and concentrated on my cock, stroking it, soaping it, almost worshipping it. She licked the length of it and played with my balls. Taking the shower head from its holder, she sprayed my groin, then turned me around, bent me over, and switched to the pulsing spray. Against my anus, the feeling was dynamite. "Don't come yet, baby," she moaned. "Wait for me."

She turned me to her, and sitting me on the little seat built into the enclosure, she ripped open a little packet and rolled a condom onto my cock. Then she sat on my lap, facing me, my dick firmly lodged in her snatch. She had the most talented vaginal muscles. She milked my cock until I came, hard, hips bucking until I could barely stay on the little seat. Still inside her, she took the shower massager and concentrated the spray on my balls.

Damn if I wasn't hard again in minutes. She leaned back and moved the spray until it was on her clit. "I'm going to come," she shrieked. "I'm going to come."

I grunted as I came again, and almost lost my hearing as she screamed, "Yes, yes, yes. Coming. Coming. Now, now."

We dried off and she collapsed on the bed, falling asleep

almost immediately. I waited for a few minutes, then decided I'd had enough so I dressed and went home.

The following day was Sunday, and I went out to pick up a newspaper and a bagel with cream cheese. There was a near riot in the bakery. Several women actually exchanged punches to see who would stand next to me in the long line. Two women handed me napkins with their phone numbers and email addresses. One actually kissed me, full on the mouth. It was like being some kind of famous rock star, and I suddenly had nothing but sympathy for the Mick Jaggers of the world. I scurried out of the shop without my bagel. Thankfully the newsstand was manned by a guy, so I could get my newspaper.

At home I had the entire day to think about all that had happened. The sex had been great, of course, but I had to admit that something had been missing. I know I should have been delighted, but mindless fucking was so—so empty. Neither Shari nor Iris had said more than a few syllables. I didn't know anything more about them than I had the week before, and they knew nothing about me.

I wondered why I wasn't thrilled. It was evident that I could have all the sex I wanted, but it was exhausting, both mentally and physically. My cock was actually sore from all the fucking I'd done in the past thirty-six hours. It should have been heaven, but it was closer to hell.

When my cell phone rang, I almost didn't answer, figuring

it was some brainwashed bimbo wanting to fuck me, but I checked the caller ID, smiled, and flipped it open. "Hi, Marny," I said. She and I had been seeing each other intermittently over the past month or so.

"Hi, Kevin. It's such a beautiful day, I thought we might go to the park and see whether we can get a tennis court."

Tennis. Not sex. She wasn't panting or making lewd suggestions. She sounded normal. Maybe my "powers" only worked in person. But what would happen to her when we got together?

I knew what I had to do.

"I'd love to, Marny. How about I meet you at the courts in an hour?"

"Great, Kevin, see you then."

I closed the phone, thought only for a moment, then booted up my computer and started Electric Pencil. I was tempted to compose a sentence to tweak things. I'd increase my bank account and ease off on the insatiable women thing.

No. The power was too enticing. I knew I didn't trust myself. I couldn't trust myself.

The cursor waited for me, blinking on a blank screen.

"Everything is back the way it was last Thursday." I almost pushed the Enter key but then added, "And Electric Pencil is now just a word processor."

I stared at my sentence for several minutes, then pushed Enter. The magic of Electric Pencil was gone.

Just to check, I typed, "There's a bagel with cream cheese on the counter in my kitchen." I pressed Enter and printed the sentence. Slowly I walked into my kitchen. No bagel. I heaved a great sigh then smiled. No bagel. Thank heaven.

One Night Out

❧

MY HUSBAND, DAVE, IS A PRETTY STRAIGHT GUY. HE'S an architect, used to putting things in organized diagrams, all the lines parallel or perpendicular. We've been married for six years with a very pleasant sex life, curtailed a bit by the birth of Cody, who's now almost five, and Lauren, eighteen months. Well, if I had to be honest, it's curtailed more than a little bit.

We'd put a hook-and-eye lock on the inside of our bedroom door, way up high so the kids couldn't play with it, to have some privacy when we want it. That gave us a little more freedom, but the closed door didn't stop sound. We're both noisy lovers, so we've had to force ourselves to be pretty quiet. Actually we'd talked about having the room soundproofed, but we couldn't do that with the chance that the kids might need us in the middle of the night.

Oh well.

Anyway, one afternoon Dave arrived home from work, looking like the cat who swallowed the canary. "Dave and Bev are going out, going out, going out. Dave and Bev are going out, my fair lady," he sang to the tune of "London Bridge."

"What's up?"

"My parents are taking the kids to their house for the night. We have reservations at Chez Marcel."

"You asked them?" We'd vowed not to burden Dave's elderly parents with our two rambunctious kids.

"They volunteered. My mom called me at work this afternoon and we got into a long discussion. They wondered why we never asked them to babysit. 'You need to get out and have some fun,' my mom said, my dad agreeing in the background."

"Wow. That's fabulous and I'm thrilled," I said. "Is this a special occasion?"

"It is now. I need some time alone with you. No rug rats. No nothing."

I was delighted. I packed a small overnight bag for Cody and Lauren, and Dave drove them over to his folks' house. At my husband's suggestion, I ran a leisurely bath and climbed in to soak, something I never had time to do.

A short while later, up to my neck in bubbles, I heard

the front door close when he returned. Moments later, Dave walked into our large bathroom with a candle in each hand. After he wordlessly put them on the vanity, he lit them, then left again, only to return with one of the kids' pails filled with ice, a bottle of champagne inside. He put it on the floor and took the two fancy tulip glasses we'd used for the bridal toast at our wedding from his pockets.

"Oh, baby," I said, my eyes filling. "We haven't used those since I found out I was pregnant the first time."

"I know, and it's sad. I mean to remedy that, at least for tonight." He winked at me. "May I join you?"

The tub was big enough for two, as we'd discovered when we first moved in a few months after Cody's birth. Dave quickly stripped and climbed in. It took a bit of arranging to get our legs in just the right places but once he was settled, he poured us two glasses of beautiful, golden, bubbly wine.

As he handed one to me, he said, "One promise. No talk about work, the kids, or the house. I want this to be for us."

We hadn't just talked in so long that it took a moment for me to come up with another topic. We sipped and began with the weather then slowly relaxed and moved on to local politics and a TV show we'd seen the weekend before. After my second glass of champagne, Dave added more hot water. "How about the Jacuzzi? Let's turn it on."

I reached behind me and flipped the switch. Jets of water pounded against our backs and sides and froth began to rise around us. I felt Dave's foot slide up the back of my thigh and his fingers play with my toes. I purred, but I'm sure he didn't hear me over the din of the jets. When his big toe found my slit and began to massage my slick flesh, a shudder ran through me.

Two can play, I thought, finding his balls with my foot. We played, teasing and sipping, for several minutes. Then Dave turned me slightly so my breasts were in the direct path of one of the water jets. It was exciting and soon there was water all over the floor.

We were both a little tipsy, so when I urged him to spread his knees in the path of another jet he threw his head back and just enjoyed. I'm sure we're not the first people to use those jets as a sex toy, but it was a first for us. After only a moment, Dave turned me so I was sitting on his lap, facing his feet. He lifted me, buoyed by the water, and lowered me onto his erection.

As he moved, I squeezed my vaginal muscles to tighten my passage. He grabbed my boobs and filled his hands with my flesh. Our mutual orgasm was quick and satisfying.

What a great start to our evening.

An hour later we were dressed in our best and seated at Chez Marcel. We feasted on steak and lobster, our conversation filled with erotic innuendos and double entendres. My dessert turned out to be a very gooey chocolate cake, while his was crème brûlée.

I scooped some icing on one finger and rubbed it over

his lips. He sucked my finger, ostensibly to lick off the fudge. He returned the favor with a dollop of pudding. After all the teasing, we were in no mood to prolong our meal, so Dave paid quickly and we rushed home.

"I'm so hot I could explode," he told me, "but I want to play a little. Are you willing?"

"Sure," I said, not really convinced that I wanted to wait to make love to him.

"All that gooey stuff gave me ideas. Come into the kitchen." Once there, he patted the counter. "Pull off your panties and sit up here," he said.

I'm no shrinking violet, and our sex life had been adventurous—before the kids. I did as he asked and settled on the counter. From one cabinet, Dave pulled out a bottle of maple syrup. My smile widened when I realized what he had in mind.

"Lean back," he said, and I propped myself on my elbows. He dribbled syrup on my pussy, then rubbed it into my folds. "Okay, the object of the game is for me to find every last drop." He paused. "With my tongue."

Sounded like a plan to me, so I spread my thighs wider.

Leaning over, his tongue explored, delving into every crevice, driving me totally crazy. Eventually he licked the insides of my pussy lips and dug deeply into my channel with his tongue. "All gone," he said and I was disappointed he was going to stop.

Not so. He stood, opened the refrigerator door, and withdrew a bottle of maraschino cherries. "With a cherry on top." He giggled. "Or inside."

As I watched, he pulled out one fruit and touched my clit with the icy globe. "Youch," I said.

"Well, let's warm it up." He pushed it into me, leaving the stem sticking out of my pussy. "Now I'll see whether I can find it."

He did and I climaxed. Hard. Hot. Screaming.

When I calmed, I said, "Okay, my turn."

We switched places, Dave now seated on the counter without his pants and shorts, his hard dick sticking straight up. I thought a minute, then got a jar of chocolate syrup and a can of whipped cream from the fridge. "I'm going to totally blow my diet," I said, "and you, too, of course."

I covered his cock and balls with fudge, then squirted whipped cream all over, topping the end of his cock with a cherry. I licked off every drop, and then sucked his cock until he came. He tasted like all the gooey sundae-makings and of his salty, tangy come.

We ended the evening in the shower and made love again, eventually collapsing into bed. "Do you think we can ask your parents for one evening a month?" I suggested.

"I'm sure we can. I just wonder why we didn't do it sooner."

Show Me

"*S*HOW ME," HE SAID.

"Show you what?" I said, not really having any doubts about what he meant.

"Show me how you pleasure yourself when you're alone."

"I don't—" I lied.

"Of course you do," he said, calm and factual. "Every woman does and I don't doubt for a moment that you do as well. I want to see."

Okay, let me back up. My name is Sherri and I'm twenty-four. I've been dating Connor for about four months and the sex has been pretty good. Although it's predictable, both of us usually climax, and what more is there than that?

Connor's a really nice guy who I met at the office. We started dating and it was maybe five dates before we ended up in bed. Our evenings usually begin with a movie or bowling or time at a watering hole with a few friends. We get home afterward, hold each other, kiss, and press our bodies together. Hands wander and quite quickly we end up on my bed, naked, making love. By the time he penetrates me, I'm wet and ready. We fuck, doze, then he goes back to his place.

This evening, we started as we usually do. We'd seen an R-rated film with lots of good, hot sex. Both of us were aroused so that, by the time we got to my living room, our kissing rapidly escalated. I pulled his shirt from the waistband of his jeans and ran my palms over the skin of his back. I love his skin, smooth and warm. He works out so I could feel his muscles as my hands roamed over his hard flesh. He pulled my sweater over my head and played with my breasts, eventually burying his face in my cleavage.

Then he picked me up and carried me into the bedroom and placed me gently on the quilt. God, I was really ready. He pulled off my jeans and the rest of my clothes until I lay there, naked. He was still dressed and I waited for him to remove his clothing and climb up beside me. Instead he sat on the edge of the bed and said, "Show me."

I'm not a stranger to sex, or to masturbation for that matter, but I've never even considered doing it where anyone, much less a totally ready guy, could see. Not a chance.

"I think you're as hungry as I am," he said, "and I've

always been curious to watch. Anyway, it's the best way for me to learn what you like."

"I like you inside of me," I said, hoping to deflect him.

"You're really wet," he said, staring at my crotch, "and I'll bet you want me right now."

I drew my legs together and pressed my thighs tightly closed. "You bet I do." I reached for him but he leaned away from me.

"If you want me, you'll have to show me first."

"Come on, Connor," I said, getting a little frustrated. "Enough."

"Not enough," he said. "It must be embarrassing as hell but I want to watch. If I don't get what I want, you won't either." He rubbed the bulge behind the zipper of his jeans. "I can always go home and take care of this myself."

I thought quickly. "Okay, I'll make a deal with you. I'll show you mine if you show me yours." I was sure he'd turn me down.

He considered, then said, "I guess you're right. Sauce for the goose and all that. Okay. Deal."

I swallowed hard. "Okay, deal?" I squeaked.

"Do you use a dildo or a vibrator?" he asked, as casual as asking me what I wanted for dinner.

In truth I had used both from time to time, but I wasn't about to tell him that. "No," I said.

"What gets you in the mood?" he continued, not letting me relax. "Erotic stories? Got any porno flicks?"

"Of course not," I said. I had a few stories I'd copied from the Internet in the bottom drawer of my dresser. *God, Sherri, you're becoming such a liar, but it's for a good cause,* I thought.

"We both know you're lying, but we'll let it go until next time. Now show me. Where do you start? Breasts? Or do you just go for the gold?"

It was beginning to look as if I had no choice so I slid my fingers through my pubic hair until I found my clit. Despite my embarrassment, I was still fully aroused so it was hard and swollen. I rubbed lightly, still upset that he was watching.

Suddenly he got up and grabbed the goose-neck floor lamp from beside my bed. He moved it over and directed the light onto my slit. "I can't see," he said, still sounding really interested. I could feel the heat from the lamp on my soaked skin. *Erotic* isn't a good enough word for the mixture of sensations: the heat, his eyes on me, my growing need.

Fuck. This was getting bad. However, now that I had my fingers in my wetness, I didn't want to stop despite his watching. He peered at me as I moved my fingers slightly.

"Like that?" he said. "I'll bet you move faster than that." He reached over and raised my chin so I had to look at him. "Please, baby, do it for me."

I let out a long sigh and gave in. I knew my body well and stroked it in just the ways that push me higher. As I rubbed, I felt his fingers join mine, mimicking my motions. I closed my eyes and just enjoyed it all. As I got closer to climax, I felt one of his fingers penetrate. "I want to feel you come," he said.

"Yes," I breathed, so far gone now there was nothing that would have slowed me down.

I felt the spasms start low in my belly and flow to my pussy. "God, I can feel it," he said, his voice raspy. "Do it."

I did. I let my orgasm take over and rubbed in all the spots that would make it better. The combination of his fingers playing with mine, and the knowledge that he was staring at me, pushed me over the edge. Like the times I insert a dildo into my pussy, his finger inside me allowed me to feel the contractions of my muscles and the twitch of my clit.

"God, baby," Connor purred. "That's so great."

I slowly came down and my body relaxed, a thin rime of sweat cooling on my skin. It might have begun as something really strange, but now I accepted the fact that I had been really aroused by the knowledge that he was watching me. I wondered whether he'd feel the same way. I took several deep breaths. "Okay, your turn," I said.

He let out a nervous chuckle. "You're not serious."

Got you, I thought. *You're as reluctant as I was. You'll be so surprised.* "A deal's a deal. I said I'd show you mine if you'd show me yours."

"A guy doesn't do that. It's silly. I want my cock inside of you when I come."

"Too bad," I said, enjoying his discomfort. What was there to be upset about after all? I'd seen him naked lots of times and he had a beautiful cock. I propped myself up on my pillows. "I'm ready for a show."

"Come on," he said, shaking his head. "You didn't really mean that."

"Of course I did." This was going to be fun. "Now strip."

He must have decided that I was serious so he stood and slowly removed his clothes. He really was gorgeous; great pecs, muscular arms, and narrow hips. His cock was only partly erect.

I patted the bed beside me and he sat. I directed the light on his crotch. "As you said, 'Sauce for the goose and all that.'" I watched his cock twitch under the heat of the lamp. "Don't touch yet," I said. "I want to see what happens before."

I gazed at him and licked my lips. It was amazing. I could watch his body react. I put one breast against his hand and that wonderful cock continued to swell. He played with my nipple, then I ran my fingernails up the inside of his thigh. His reaction was immediate. "Show me," I said.

He let out a long breath, obviously now resigned.

He ran his fingers through my pussy to gather my wetness, then began to touch his cock. I saw his fingers curl around the hard rod and slide from base to tip. Then he used one finger to gather his precome and use the additional lubrication to assist his ministrations. His strokes ran the length of his cock and, remembering how good it had felt to have his fingers join mine, I placed my hand over his. A slight shiver echoed through his body.

Gradually his hand picked up the pace and I heard his

breathing rate increase. His eyes closed and his head fell back. Faster and faster until, with a long groan, I saw semen spurt from his cock and dribble onto my hand and his.

After we cleaned up, he crawled in beside me and we curled into each other. For the first time, he stayed until the next morning.

After the Wedding

HE WEDDING AND ALL THE FESTIVITIES THAT LED UP TO it had been wonderful for many reasons. It had been great for Connie to see her old college roommate, Laura, again and to meet her fiancé and now-husband, Brett. Connie had introduced them to her yearlong live-in, Mark. The place was spectacular and the rehearsal dinner was filled with laughter and reminiscences. The small ceremony had taken place on the patio of an intimate little inn in the mountains with only four couples, an aunt and uncle of the groom, and Laura's parents, who lived in a neighboring town, in attendance.

The dinner afterward was filled with more joy and several celebratory toasts. By the end of the meal, and the dancing that followed, Connie was feeling quite mellow and Mark was his usual amorous self, being especially sexual after a few martinis.

Giggling, the newlyweds adjourned to their room around eleven and, after bidding everyone a good night, Mark and Connie followed a little while later. They stripped off their finery and, still in their underwear, stretched out on the big double bed to discuss the wedding. After only a few minutes, they discovered that they could hear what was going on in the next room, the one obviously occupied by the bridal couple.

"I can't believe we're truly married," they heard Laura say. Her raspy voice was easy to recognize.

"And now we can fool around legally," Brett replied.

There was a gasp and a giggle. *"Brett, cut that out."*

"Why?" he said, eliciting another gasp.

"These walls aren't very thick. I'm afraid anyone in the next room can hear."

Connie looked at Mark, then whispered, "Should we let them know we're listening?"

"Not a chance," Mark said with a wink. "This is just too juicy."

"Don't you dare tease him tomorrow morning."

Mark just winked again.

"It's not up to you to wonder," Brett said. *"That's my department."*

"Of course."

"You didn't say those words right, you know," Brett growled.

"I'm sorry. Of course, sir." There was a pause. *"I'll try to be better from now on."*

"What the hell is that all about?" Connie hissed.

Mark put his finger against his lips for silence.

"You'd better be," Brett said.

Another giggle. *"I'll try harder."*

"That's not good enough. I think, since it's a special day, I'll only give you five for your error."

"Five what?" Connie whispered.

"Panties off," they heard Brett say.

After a few moments, Connie heard a smack and her eyes widened. "Is he doing what I think he's doing?" She was amazed and, surprisingly, aroused.

Another smack. *"That's two."*

"I think he's giving her a spanking."

Mark slipped his hand between Connie's legs. "And it makes you wet, doesn't it?"

Another smack. *"That's three."*

Connie remained silent, but the sounds in the next room were driving her pussy crazy. Mark continued to lightly stroke her clit through her panties.

Another smack. *"That's four."*

Connie could barely control her breathing. This was so bad. She'd never realized that she could be turned on by pain, but there was no denying it.

Another smack. *"That's five."*

"Did you bring some lotion?" Laura said. *"You really pack a wallop."*

"Of course." Brett's voice has changed to a soft purr.

There followed several minutes of whispering, then the rhythmic sounds of lovemaking.

"Holy cow," Connie whispered. "I never thought that Laura would be into violence like that."

"It's not really violence," Mark said, still stroking Connie's clit. His voice was barely above a whisper, knowing Laura and Brett could hear him and Connie as easily as they'd heard them. "It's just that sometimes people find pain enhances sexual pleasure."

"Do you?"

"Find it exciting? I didn't think so, but it's difficult to deny that listening aroused me. Would it excite me for us to do something like that? I don't know. We've never tried." He paused. "There's also giving and receiving. I don't know how I'd feel about either spanking you or being spanked."

"Well," Connie said, trying to deny the obvious, "I don't think it would be good for us."

Mark chuckled. "Your soaked panties say different."

Connie glanced at her boyfriend's briefs and the swollen bulge beneath. She reached over and squeezed. "You look like the idea appeals to you, too. However, don't try anything like that here. We know how thin the walls are."

"Would you be willing for me to try a slap on your ass from time to time?"

Connie was really embarrassed, but she and Mark had always been truthful about their sexual preferences. "I don't really know. Until tonight something like that has always seemed beyond the pale."

After a long and passionate kiss, Mark pulled Connie's bra aside and licked her swollen nipple. Connie had always been a noisy lover, but now she knew she had to keep silent. Laura and Brett would be able to hear.

They stripped, fondled and kissed, nibbled and licked for long minutes, then Mark helped Connie straddle his rigid erection. As she lowered her dripping pussy onto Mark's cock, he pinched her butt, hard. She gasped, then silently rode him until they were both panting and covered with sweat.

The bed bounced against the wall but they were both beyond caring. "Oh, God," Connie hissed. "Oh, God!" She rode him, taking her pleasure. She slid one hand between them and rubbed herself, then reached behind her and grabbed Mark's balls. She couldn't get enough of him.

As she was about to come, Mark pinched her again. She climaxed, trying to keep her moans under control. She felt her boyfriend bucking beneath her and almost immediately after her climax, he spurted into her.

"Holy shit," Mark whispered. "You were a tiger tonight."

She laughed. "Yeah, I guess I was."

"That little bit of pain really lit your fuse."

"Maybe when we have a little more privacy, we could talk about it."

"Talk and more. After this, I've got a few ideas."

"Naughty, erotic ideas, I hope."

"Oh, yeah."

"Good night you two," Laura called from the next room. *"I guess we'll all sleep well tonight."*

Almost asleep, Mark mumbled, "I guess we will."

Madam's Brothel: Option 1

⸙

CURRENTLY EMILY'S SEX LIFE STANK. SHE WOULDN'T admit it to anyone, of course. As a matter of fact, when people at work asked about her love life, she'd smile enigmatically and return to her computer.

She'd had several boyfriends, two of whom had lived with her, but none had lasted more than six months. Boring sex, even then. Predictable and ordinary, and what was worse, she'd known it. She'd settled. She often wondered what the rest of the world was like, sex-wise, but at the moment, there didn't seem to be any possibilities for her to find out.

She had a few friends, of course, of both sexes, but they spent time at bars and clubs where she usually felt totally out of place. So she spent more and more of her off-work time at home, playing online computer games. Oh sure, she'd tried some of the dating sites, but it had all been for naught. She was lonely, but didn't know what to do about it, so each evening, after making herself a sandwich or frozen dinner, she'd take her plate, along with a beer, into her bedroom, settle at her tiny workstation, and turn on her computer.

While logged onto Games, Games, Games one evening, she noticed a new adventure game housed in a special section labeled "Adults Only." She'd never been to the adults-only area, but she found herself intrigued so she clicked on it. When she'd logged on for the first time, she'd been asked her age so the system knew she was in her midtwenties. The game was called "For Lovers," and she read the screen on how to play.

Your quest is to find the Ruby Ring of Ultimate Sexual Pleasure by moving through various rooms in a very exclusive brothel, until you reach the treasure. If you've got enough love points, you can claim the ruby ring.

Emily loved adventure games. She'd played a zillion, but this one seemed different from others she'd mastered, maybe more exciting. *Great,* she thought, *a new experience.* She clicked on Start. To begin, she wandered around the virtual town, gathering life points and money, finally finding the Key of Experience to get her into Madam's Brothel, the start of her quest.

Once inside, she saw bosomy women dressed in scanty outfits and hunky guys in Speedos, all waiting for customers. As she moved her mouse around, names appeared over the characters: Suzanne Sunrise, MaryLee Dreamboat, Carl Creative, and many more. If she clicked on one, he or she made a little speech about how she should spend her money and choose his or her character to go into the Love Nest with. *Love Nest?* She assumed that was the room where animated characters made out and she could watch. Hokey, yes, but it might be fun to see how the other half lived. Could she do it? She sat back and gazed at the animated crowd. *God, if only there were a real and totally anonymous place like in this game.* She'd never actually consider making it with a paid guy, but if she could . . . She could ask for all the things she'd never done, and her partner wouldn't make fun of her inexperience.

Finally, she settled on Randy Pornstar. She loved the name, and his shaggy blond hair and magnificent body appealed to her. He was dressed in her favorite sexy-guy outfit: jeans, unbuttoned at the waist, and no shirt. There was an arrow of hair on his flat belly that disappeared beneath the zipper. And his feet were bare. He had great toes. God, she must be hard up if she thought his *toes* were great. She looked at the exciting lump beneath his fly. Even though he was an animated image, her mind was certainly directed to the right places.

She clicked on his image and together they walked into

the Love Nest. She looked down and saw what were supposed to be her own feet and was surprised to see that they were wearing sneakers just like hers. After he opened the door for her, Randy reached down and lifted one of her cartoon feet to pull off her sock and shoe, then did the same for the other foot. She felt compelled to take her hand off her mouse and remove her own footwear.

Although it was all in fun and pretty silly, even on a fourteen-inch screen, it felt a little illicit. Inside the room it was as though he was looking her right in the eye. "Have you ever been here before?" he asked, the sound quite realistic.

She clicked on No.

"What would you like to do?"

A list appeared on the screen, overlaying the view of the room.

1. Oral sex receiving
2. Oral sex performing
3. Anal sex
4. Light bondage—being bound
5. Light bondage—binding me
6. More options

Damn if this didn't feel real. She thought a moment, then clicked on Option 1. She guessed that she'd see an image of Randy, seeming to play with her.

"I'm glad you selected that option," Randy said through

the computer's speakers. "I love licking a beautiful pussy. Stretch out on the bed." On the screen she saw herself stretch out on a satiny bed. She could look around the room, hear the soft music, almost smell the scented candles flickering on the nightstand. She looked down and saw her animated, naked legs. *Strange coincidence*, she thought. *There's a little mole on my left knee, just like the one I have in real life.*

Randy Pornstar positioned himself between her thighs and she could almost feel his hot breath through her pants. Without thinking, she quickly pulled off her jeans, sat back on her desk chair, and gazed at the almost realistic-looking scene. She could swear she felt it. His fingers parting her outer lips, his mouth licking her clit, his tongue flicking over her swollen flesh. She heard him hum and felt the buzz in her groin. Her flesh was wet and puffy. Her pussy twitched as he kept up his expert ministrations on the screen.

His fingers found her and she actually felt him slide two inside her, slowly withdrawing and filling until she thought she'd die from the pleasure of it. It seemed as if she actually experienced it as he nibbled on her and bit lightly until the sensations overwhelmed her.

She came—actually climaxed—just from watching the screen and imagining. It *was* imagination, right? After her orgasm, her hands shook and she was unable to use her mouse, so she just rested against the back of her chair and trembled.

"That was really good for you," Randy Pornstar said. "I'm so glad."

"How do you know that?" she said aloud.

"I just do," the computer speaker said.

"What the hell?"

"Don't ask silly questions," Randy said. "Just come back tomorrow. I'll be waiting."

Madam's Brothel: Option 3

✣

*T*HE FOLLOWING EVENING, EMILY HURRIED HOME FROM work. She grabbed a burger and fries at the McDonald's on her corner and rushed up to her apartment. She'd brought her laptop home from work so she could log on to Games, Games, Games while lying on her bed. It would be so much more comfortable. She stripped off her jeans, plumped the pillows behind her, and sat on the bed. She clicked on "For Lovers," and quickly amassed the needed life points and money, then retrieved the key to Madam's Brothel and went inside. There were about the same number of men and women in the room but she wasn't interested. Randy was waiting for her, and once she'd selected him, they retired to the Love Nest.

"I enjoyed last evening," he said, "and I hope you did, too."

How the hell does the game know I was here last evening? She considered, then figured it out. Relieved, she thought, *This game must leave a cookie on my computer to tell it that I was here last evening. That must be it.*

Then she reasoned further. It couldn't be that. She had been on her desktop computer the previous evening. Right, but she'd logged in with the same user name. Fears finally eased, she let out a long breath.

"Don't worry about small things," Randy said. "What would you like to do tonight?"

Again the list appeared on the screen.

1. Oral sex receiving
2. Oral sex performing
3. Anal sex
4. Light bondage—being bound
5. Light bondage—binding me
6. More options

She clicked on Option 1 and again she climaxed, more explosively than she had the previous evening. When she finally turned off the computer, she was exhausted.

The pattern continued for several evenings, with Emily rushing home to experience more of Option 1. Each night it seemed to get better.

Finally, after about a week, she was feeling daring. She

moved her mouse from the first link on the menu, and clicked on Option 3.

"Wonderful," Randy said. "I hoped you would move on to something more creative. I love fucking a wonderful woman's tight ass." His smile was warm and supportive. Almost loving. "You've never done Option 3 before, have you."

It wasn't a question. She didn't want to have to admit her innocence, but as he seemed to be able to do, he sensed her reluctance and said, "It's all right. You don't have to say anything."

Her long sigh was her only answer.

"First you need to take everything off." She saw clothing tossed around the Love Nest on the screen, and she couldn't resist the temptation to remove her jeans, shirt, and undies, then settle back on the bed.

"You've got great tits," Randy said, seeming to gaze at her body. "May I play with them first?"

"God, yes," she said aloud, already aroused. She actually felt fingers tweaking her erect nipples. She cupped her breasts and saw hands cupping the large tits of the figure on the screen. Randy bent down and she watched him take one bud in his mouth. She felt the tugging but accepted the fact that it was her own fingers playing with her flesh. When she moved her hands to her sides though, she still felt the tug of his sucking. It felt so good that she didn't dwell on her confusion.

Randy Pornstar moved back and said, "Let's play a little more. I know what you selected, what you want, and from now on you don't have to say anything. I understand everything and I'll make it good for you, I promise. Now curl up on your side."

Willing to play along, Emily put the laptop on the bed beside her and did as he asked. *What will I feel? After all, it's just a computer game.* But then she had experienced many things so far.

Suddenly she was wary. Anal sex. She'd never considered trying it before, but this way there was nothing to worry about. Right? She could experiment without consequences. This wasn't real, after all.

On the screen, Randy held up a slender dildo. "I'm not going to penetrate your beautiful, virgin ass with my cock just yet. That will wait for another evening when you've adjusted to this kind of game. For now I'll just use this."

As she watched the computer screen, Randy poured a generous dollop of lubricant on the dildo and sensuously rubbed it all over. Emily's flesh was tingling. As Randy moved behind her avatar, she felt hands on her ass cheeks. "It's okay, honey," he said, "just relax. I know you'll enjoy this. And if you want to rub your clit, do it. I love to watch."

The sensation of cold, slippery fingers on her ass was almost real. Almost, almost real. Then she felt penetration. She looked over her shoulder to assure herself that she was still alone in her room. How was this happening? She had no idea, but she was in such ecstasy that she forgot to worry about it.

As the dildo slipped into her ass, she felt her clit swell to mammoth proportions. When she reached between her legs, it was as though she were on fire. The fullness in her ass somehow transferred the sensation to her cunt. "That's it, honey," Randy said from behind her. Sound? Behind her? "Rub your clit. I want to watch you make yourself come."

Her heart was pounding so loud that she could barely hear him. "Yes, like that. Show me how you can come with me fucking your ass with this toy."

The dildo pulled out, then thrust inside her ass again. She rubbed her clit, and as she had on the previous evenings, she came. "That's right, baby, come. Hard. Fast. Feel the spasms throughout your body. I can feel them on my toy. Do it."

It was as though her orgasm lasted for minutes, even hours. She lost track of time as her body clenched and relaxed over and over.

Finally she felt the dildo withdraw and she slipped into a light doze. When she awoke, she glanced at the computer screen. Her colorful screen saver wove its patterns through the black background. The time on the tray told her she'd been out for a few hours. She moved the mouse and the screen saver dissolved into her desktop. Should she go back to Madam's Brothel? Not tonight. Right now she was too well fucked.

Tomorrow.

Tomorrow another option. Or maybe this one again. She'd decide then. Totally content, she pulled a blanket over herself and went to sleep.

Madam's Brothel:
Option 7

❧

$\mathcal{F}$OR THE NEXT MONTH, EMILY WAS OBSESSED WITH Madam's Brothel. She turned down invitations to go out with her office buddies, rushed home from visits to her parents or her sister's family, and every evening she went into the Love Nest with Randy. Occasionally she selected Option 3, but most of her time was spent enjoying Randy's talent with oral sex. Her body had become tuned to his kind of lovemaking, and she enjoyed it more than she'd ever enjoyed "real" lovemaking. She realized that she was supposed to be searching for the Ruby Ring of Ultimate Sexual Pleasure, whatever that was, but she refused to even consider leaving the brothel.

One evening, before she selected an option, Randy asked,

"Aren't you even curious about the other possibilities? Option 6?"

Usually she didn't even look at the list. When she entered Madam's, she knew what she wanted. Now she reread the menu.

1. Oral sex receiving
2. Oral sex performing
3. Anal sex
4. Light bondage—being bound
5. Light bondage—binding me
6. More options

More options. She had been in such a hurry, so content with her selections, that she'd overlooked the additional possibilities. What were the other options? When she clicked on Option 6 a new menu appeared.

7. Mutual masturbation
8. Toys
9. Threesomes—with two men
10. Threesomes—with another couple
11. Light pain—spanking
12. Water sports
13. The ultimate orgy

Water sports? She vaguely knew what that was and quickly accepted the fact that she wasn't interested. "Don't discount things before you've tried them," Randy said, reading her mind as usual.

"Not right now," she said. Spanking? How would that work? She knew that she was able to feel things through some kind of psychic connection with Randy, but spanking? There was no way she could get sufficiently into that to truly feel it.

She'd never seen Randy without his jeans and now she was curious, so she clicked on Option 7.

"Mmm," he purred. "You want me to perform for you? And you'll join me, of course. Great. I can't wait." He reached behind him. "Let's take our time." He showed her a bottle of massage oil. "Got any?"

"In the bathroom, I think." She remembered that Gary, a former roommate, had bought some in his short-lived creative period.

"Good. Get it."

When she returned with the dust-covered bottle, he said, "Sit on the edge of the bed. I wouldn't want to get your lovely chintz comforter all oily."

She looked at her bed. She had a chintz comforter. How the hell did the character on a computer screen know these things? She accepted it as she'd slowly accepted the rest of the experience. "Whatever."

In the Love Nest, Randy poured oil in his palm and began to slather it all over his shoulders and chest, sensuously stroking his deeply tanned skin. She watched and willed herself to be patient. Recently their lovemaking had become easy and quick. Now she'd take her time and revel in the sights and sensations. "This feels sexy," he purred. "Now you do some."

She pulled off her shirt and bra and filled her cupped palm with oil. Slowly, with only a little embarrassment, she rubbed her hands over her shoulders, then her breasts. "You have such lovely breasts," Randy said. "Stroke them while I watch. Play with your nipples."

She did.

"Pull them, tweak the tips, squeeze."

She followed his instructions. Yes. She did the things that felt really good, playing with her tits and enjoying the increasing pitch of her arousal.

As she watched, Randy's eyes seemed to follow her hands. She saw that he was rubbing his belly, sliding his fingers beneath the fabric of his jeans. She stared and smiled.

"Ahh, you like," he said, unzipping the rest of the way, then slowly, sensuously sliding the pants down over his hips and kicking them aside. He wore no underwear. She could see that his beautiful cock was fully erect. It wasn't tremendous or phony-looking, just rigid, jutting from its nest of hair. "Now you."

She removed the rest of her clothing and stretched out on the bed, the computer at her side.

"Good. Now watch my hand."

As she stared at his erection, the camera, or whatever it was that controlled the characters in the room, zoomed in on his hands and his cock. He sensuously stroked himself from base to tip, then back again. It was so realistic that she could see the veins and arteries, the purple head, his fingers squeezing and releasing. She heard his groan and her fingers slid to her pussy. By now she knew all the best places to stroke, and she pushed herself higher and higher as she watched Randy's hands.

Now one hand rubbed his penis and the other cupped his balls. She was almost mesmerized as he stroked, and she stroked. "I'm going to come," he moaned.

"Me, too," she whispered.

"Then let's come together." He rubbed, his thick, heavy breathing audible through the speakers. "Just another moment."

Panting, heart pounding, the sound of blood rushing in her ears, she rubbed, found her clit, and touched it lightly.

He almost purred. "Another moment, another moment, yes, now. NOW!"

As she stared, thick gobs of semen jetted from his cock. She came, too, her entire body trembling.

She watched him collapse onto the bed behind him. Replete she clicked off the computer and fell asleep.

Madam's Brothel:
Option 8

❦

*A*S TIME PASSED, EMILY REALIZED THAT SHE WAS BECOM-
ing more adventurous about sex, even if it was only in a virtual environment. Never before had she experienced so many
new sensations. More and more she was able to participate
in what she was feeling and seeing, sharing great sex with
Randy. They'd played with blindfolds—she'd applied one
and then listened as Randy told her what to do. She'd gotten a transparent shower curtain, and with the computer on
the toilet seat, she'd performed for him, massaging her body
with a soapy sponge, then a rough loofah. She'd mounted a
mirror on the wall of her bedroom and watched both herself and Randy during lovemaking. Day by day the psychic
connection between them got stronger. She felt everything

more and more directly, more and more deeply. Why, she lamented, wasn't he real?

One evening she even spoke to the screen, and Randy. "I want you to be real," she said. "I want you here with me when I get home from work."

"Be patient," he said. "I know you'll find some way to work with it. What about trying to find the Ruby Ring of Ultimate Sexual Pleasure? It might help you."

"Why would I want that? I've got just about everything I want right here." Then she realized that she was discussing things with a computer animation. That was depressing in a way, but when she got really down about it, she grabbed herself by the scruff of her neck and told herself to enjoy what there was and not to be sad about what there wasn't.

"Right," Randy said. "Just revel in all your new pleasures. How about doing something new this evening?" The menu flashed onto the screen. "I've got a few toys you might enjoy," he said, grinning.

   7. Mutual masturbation

   8. Toys

   9. Threesomes—with two men

 10. Threesomes—with another couple

 11. Light pain—spanking

 12. Water sports

 13. The ultimate orgy

Option 8. She had complete faith in Randy's ability to make her senses react to whatever he did, so she clicked on Option 8. "While we're at it, why don't you invite one of the others to join us here in the Love Nest? You'd be amazed at what clever things we could do."

Threesome? Option 9? She couldn't imagine sharing Randy with anyone else—but having another man with them? That might be fun. She hesitated. "Two options at the same time?"

"Sure, why not? We really need to further your education and have some fun," the speakers intoned. "Go back outside and pick a man to join us."

Did she truly want to do this? What the hell! It was all in fun and it existed only in her imagination anyway. No one else would know. No one else would judge her. And judge her for what?

She used her mouse to walk her screen-self back into the main room and clicked over each of the men there. Each one gave a little speech about how much he could add to her delight. Finally she selected a character known only as Toy Boy. He was shorter than Randy but stockier, with a weightlifter's body and a wide smile. He wore jeans and a vest covered with bulging pockets. She had a pretty good idea what those pockets contained and her pussy twitched in anticipation.

He preceded her into the Love Nest. "Fabulous," Randy said.

"You told me about her," Toy Boy said. "I can't wait."

"Will you trust us?" Randy said. "We'll play with some new stuff. If anything isn't enjoyable, just say 'no more' and we'll switch to something else. Fair?"

She nodded and they both seemed to know she'd agreed.

"Your clothing needs to come off," Toy Boy said to her and she quickly complied, then put the computer on the bed beside her.

Toy Boy looked at Randy on the screen. "You told me she was fabulous and I can believe it."

"I have good taste," Randy said. As if he'd chosen her rather than the other way around.

"Good choice. Okay, Emily, lie back and watch," Toy Boy said.

He'd called her Emily. He knew her name. Amazing.

Toy Boy opened one pocket and pulled out a long, thick dildo. "This one vibrates, and this collar," he said, showing her a thickened section about halfway down its length, "does some delicious things." He put it on the table beside him. From another pocket he drew a slender dildo with a wide flange at the base. "An anal probe," he said.

"I know how much you like that kind of play," Randy said. She couldn't deny it.

"And these should add to the sensations." From a lower pocket Toy Boy pulled a chain with what looked like clothes-pins attached. "Randy, you've got the best connection with her. How about you do the honors?"

She looked down both in reality and on the screen and watched him tease her nipples until they were hard and tight. Then he clipped the pins onto first one, then the other. The clips were there on the screen, all right. She looked down at her hard nipples. No clips, but the pain she felt was very real. She took in a breath to ask Randy to take them off, then the pain receded a bit and arrows of pleasure went directly to her cunt. Toy Boy pulled on the chain connecting them and the delight intensified.

Toy Boy flipped a switch on the vibrator to show her how it worked, turned it off, and gave it to Randy, who pushed it into her already sopping pussy. Then Toy Boy flipped the switch on the base and the buzzing began. Her hips bucked. "Wow, she's so responsive," Toy Boy said.

"I told you," Randy responded, grinning with pleasure.

She loved the compliments, even if it was just from two animated characters on a computer screen.

She wanted to close her eyes and savor the ecstasy, but she didn't want to lose the connection with Randy and Toy Boy. "Now this one," Toy Boy said, slathering some lube onto the anal probe. While Randy played with the vibrator in her cunt, Toy Boy said, "Knees up." When she complied, he slid the slender staff into her ass. It was too much. Hips thrashing, fists contracting, toes curling, she climaxed. Until then she'd been able to control her screams, but tonight she couldn't. The power of her climax made her unable to control anything.

"She's quite something," Toy Boy said. Then he looked at her. "Next time choose Option 13. Then we can have the greatest time."

Option 13: The ultimate orgy. Maybe she would. Maybe she would.

Madam's Brothel: Option 13

❧

THREE MONTHS HAD PASSED SINCE EMILY FIRST FOUND Madam's Brothel and Randy. She visited almost every evening and he was always there waiting for her. When she thought about what he did during the daytime, she actually experienced a twinge of jealousy, but when she considered that, she laughed. Jealousy? Of a character in an online game, an animation?

She had to admit, though, there was a connection. A physic connection. He made her feel things she never expected to feel, pleasures of the flesh, as the romance novels she enjoyed might say. She no longer felt embarrassed about any of the games they'd played.

"Let's celebrate your three-month anniversary, love," Randy said. "Choose Option 13."

She gazed at the menu.

13. The ultimate orgy

She thought a lot about Option 13 and it tickled her fancy as it wouldn't have three months before. Now she thought she was ready for anything. Anything? There might be women who desired her. Men who wanted to spank her. Water sports. Was she ready?

Emily knew she could always say no to an activity, and she trusted the characters in the drama to obey her wishes. Trusted? Cartoon characters? All she had to do was turn off her computer and they'd be gone. But it was so difficult for her to think of them in those terms. In the past weeks she'd invited many of them into threesome scenarios, and on the rare occasion that things had gone too far, they'd always stopped when she said so.

Of course they did, she told herself. *They're characters in a computer game. They aren't real!* But they felt real, she argued with herself. They peopled her evenings. They talked to her, made her sense things, feel things. They knew her and what she liked. How? She'd long given up trying to solve that mystery.

Option 13. She clicked on it.

"Wonderful," Randy said. After she stripped, he reached

out and she saw him take her hand. Together they walked through a doorway into the Hot Tub Room. She'd noticed it on one of her early visits but had paid no attention. Now they were inside.

The party was in full swing. The room was dominated by a multiperson hot tub, bubbling, vapor drifting toward the ceiling. Several animated couples were making out. Fondling. Sucking. Breasts bobbing. Erections sticking up from the heated water. One woman had her arms extended on the edge, and Emily noticed that her wrists were tied there. A man on either side of her was sucking on her large breasts while a third man stood, his penis in her mouth.

Toy Boy sat on the ledge that half surrounded the tub, grinning, a dildo or vibrator in each hand, the heads of the women on each side of him thrown back, moans issuing from their open mouths.

"Join me?" Randy asked as he climbed the ladder and stepped into the hot water.

"Sure," she said and sensed the heated water on her body.

As she settled, one woman winked at her and said, "I'm Georgia, and I have to tell you that I'm amazed. You sure have grown in the past three months."

Boy, had she, but how in the world did Georgia know that? She was, though, part of the game. She had to stop thinking of them as real people. "Thanks to Randy."

"No, love," Randy said, "thanks to yourself. Take all the credit. You deserve it."

She didn't want to challenge him so she nodded. Georgia made her way over, sat beside her, reached beneath the water, and tweaked one nipple. A woman's hands on her body? What the hell. It didn't feel any different than a man's.

Randy sat on her other side and played with her other breast. Then the two lifted her so she was sitting on the ledge, feet still in the bubbling water. One mouth on each tit. She was in heaven. "Close your eyes," Randy said, "and see whether you can guess whose mouth is giving you pleasure."

Close her eyes? She'd never been sure what would happen if she stopped looking at the screen, but she did as he asked and the mouths were still there. Then someone moved between her spread legs and a tongue flicked over her clit. Her juices mixed with the water from the tub and her excitement grew.

She was tempted to look but didn't want the mouth to stop sucking on her clit . . . Randy said, "Keep them closed."

Higher and higher she climbed, one pair of lips on her breast, one on her clit. When a finger penetrated her soaked cunt and another slid into her ass, she came, barely able to keep her seat beside the tub. She braced her palms on the ledge, curling her fingers over the edge to try to keep her balance.

As she regained her breath, she realized that there was something solid beneath her fingertips. She groped beneath the ledge and pulled out a golden ring with a bright red stone. "She found it!" one man yelled, and there was a round of applause.

"Is this it?" she asked. "The Ruby Ring of Ultimate Sexual Pleasure?"

"That's it, love," Randy said. "It means you get to join us."

"Sorry?"

"Having found the ring, you get to become a character in our game." Suddenly she was in the Hot Tub Room. It was real. Randy was real. She was no longer in her bedroom. She reached out and touched Randy, really touched him for the first time. The ledge was solid beneath her hands. The water was hot and she kicked, splashing Toy Boy and the women beside him. Everyone was laughing and congratulating her.

"How . . . ?"

Randy took a seat beside her. Flesh-and-blood Randy. "Actually, my name's Marco," he said, "and Toy Boy's real name is Pierre. Everyone here has another life during the day, but each of us found the Ruby Ring of Ultimate Sexual Pleasure. You can now join us in here anytime you want to, just by holding on to the ring and thinking yourself here. You get to pick a name and participate in whatever kind of sex you want, with whomever you want."

"With the folks here?"

"Yes, and with the new people who find our game room. You can teach, if you want, or just play."

She clutched the ring. "What about off hours? Are you real? Are you Marco or Randy?"

Randy laughed and kissed her for the first time. "Funny. We've done so much together, but we've never kissed." His lips played over hers and his tongue filled her mouth. "Actually, Marco lives just a few blocks from you."

"Can we meet for real?"

He grinned. "Yes. Out there, in here, it's all the same. Now that you've found the ring, we can have dinner together, get to know each other. You might find that I'm a great sex partner, but not anyone you'd like to be with outside of Madam's Brothel. Or we might just hit it off."

"That remains to be seen, doesn't it?"

"It certainly does."

Unintended Consequences

⁂

AUDREY DIDN'T KNOW WHY SHE BOUGHT THE LITTLE
jar in the thrift store, but something about it appealed to
her. Only a few inches tall, the jar, or bottle, or whatever, was
brass, with intricate, swirly carvings around the base and a
wide lip at the top.

She had a shadowbox on her wall and knew it would look
just perfect next to the small, ruby glass bud vase. Sadly, as
she put the small object on the narrow wooden shelf, the
little vase fell and smashed on the floor.

"Shit, shit, shit!" she muttered, heading for the kitchen
to get the dustpan and brush. "Damn and double damn!"
Returning, she swept the floor and dusted the shards of broken glass from the brass. Before she replaced it on the shelf,

she rubbed the surface to try to get a little extra shine. Suddenly, she saw a wisp of smoke drift upward from the inside. "What the hell?" she said.

"You know, Audrey you shouldn't curse like that." The voice was—well, the best way she could describe it was *large*.

"What the fuck are you?" she spat.

"I guess genies are a little passé now, but that's what I am." Slowly a large figure materialized looking like the friendly genie in *Aladdin*. "Right here, right now, and ready to grant you three wishes."

"You've got to be kidding."

"Nope," he said, sounding a bit like Robin Williams. "Scout's honor." He extended two chubby fingers and saluted.

"Riiight!"

"You have three wishes. If you don't care to use them, I can always give them to someone else."

Really! Did he expect her to believe him? "Come on, be real. You slipped out of a brass bottle I bought at Goodwill, for God's sake. I didn't find it on a beach or have it given to me by a wizard."

"I can't speak for where or how you got it. I've been stuffed in here for, well, to me it seems like forever." He paused then tilted his head to one side quizzically. "What century is it anyway?"

"The twenty-first," she replied without thinking.

"Already? I was just in the middle of the French Revolution. They say time flies when you're having fun." He slowly shook his head. "Actually I wasn't having any fun at all."

She snorted an exasperated breath. "Okay, let's say I believe you, or at least I believe that you believe. Let's just give it a test. Fix my broken vase."

"That's a really puny wish," the genie said. "You should think before you use up one third of your gift."

Audrey grinned. "Got you. You can't do it. I knew it. I don't know who or what you are but just beat it."

"If you really want to spend your wish that way . . ." He waved his hand and the little ruby glass vase was back on the shelf in one piece, right where it had been.

Audrey put her hand over her suddenly pounding heart and dropped onto her sofa. It was true. She actually had a genie all her own. "Holy . . ."

"Hey, Audrey, no more cursing. That's my personal wish and it doesn't use any of yours." He stood tall and cleared his throat. "Okay, let's get down to brass tacks, as it were. There are a few wish rules." He held up one finger. "You can't wish for more wishes. Several of my previous owners tried and merely wasted a wish."

He extended another finger. "Each new person who owns me gets three wishes, but you can't just give me away to a friend, let them have wishes, then get me back. My bottle has to be owned by someone who doesn't know its power."

A third finger waved in the air. "You have one week to use them or lose them."

A fourth finger. "Oh, and you can't tell anyone about these wishes. It's only between you and me. No outside advice."

He looked Audrey in the eye and smiled. "And this last isn't a rule, but some advice from someone"—he pointed to himself—"me, who's been granting wishes for many centuries. Hold the last wish aside just in case. Sometimes, if you're not careful enough about what you wish for, you need to undo something."

"That's it?"

"That's it. Give it lots of thought. Everything has consequences. Lots of money brings the tax man. World peace, well, it's a noble goal but that kind of peace lasts for about a nanosecond until someone decides he or she wants something the country next door has."

He shrugged. "It's all been tried. Health for the world's people? Puts doctors, hospitals, and insurance companies out of business. Wrecks the economy. Long life? Excess population, food shortages. The wish business isn't as easy as you might think."

Audrey huffed out a breath. "I see what you mean." She thought for a minute, then said, "You're right. I'd better think about this carefully."

"Good girl. You have two wishes left, and you'll want to save one until the last day in case of unintended consequences. So think seriously about how to spend the one you can use." Then, with a wisp of smoke, he disappeared.

Audrey thought of nothing else all evening. She didn't

sleep, just considered her wish. Over a bowl of Cheerios the following morning, she finally made a decision. She was in her early thirties and had had few boyfriends. She didn't think she was homely, just ordinary. She wasn't interested in the things guys liked: cars, computer adventure games, naked women. She didn't know even the basics of how to talk to a guy. And she was skinny, all elbows and shoulder blades, and no boobs. Really no boobs. A guy had once commented that her chest looked like two raisins on a board. Another guy had told her that he wanted to hang her bra on the mantel at Christmas so Santa could fill it up. *I want boobs!* she thought. *And guys. I want a sex life.*

"Genie," she said aloud at about eight. "I think I've made up my mind, but I need help in framing the wish so I don't get any unintended consequences."

The genie appeared. "You don't have to say it. I know what you're thinking. You want to be attractive to guys, both in body and in attitude. You want to know how to meet them, talk to them, get them to want to take you to bed. Right? And you want big breasts."

"Exactly."

"Okay, I've got it. And so have you. Check yourself out in the mirror."

Audrey dashed into the bedroom and looked at herself in the full-length mirror on the closet door. She had boobs. Tits. Knockers. And cleavage. She sighed and almost wept with joy. "I've always wanted cleavage."

"Now you've got it."

She continued to gaze at herself. "My waist is slender." She pulled off her jeans. "And I've got great legs."

She yanked off her T-shirt and pulled off the push-up bra she found beneath. "Sh—"

"Watch the language."

"I mean, gosh. Look." She turned this way and that, admiring her new body.

Finally, breathless, she put her clothing back on. "What about talking to guys?"

"I'll give you a few pointers when you get home from work, and you can go to someplace local and try out your new personality. Count on it."

"Work! Damn. I mean drat."

She checked her watch and quickly realized that she had only five minutes to make her bus. Grabbing her purse, she ran out the door.

On the bus, she sat next to the good-looking business type she frequently ran into. New personality. Okay, genie. Do your stuff. "Good morning," she said to the guy, his nose buried in his newspaper.

He looked up. "Well, good morning to you. You're very cheery this morning."

"I guess I am." She heard the genie in her mind. *You can't tell anyone about me.* "It's such a beautiful morning, why not celebrate it?"

"Why not, indeed. And the Yankees won last evening and Boston lost."

Baseball? Genie! *It's okay to ask questions. Men like to teach.* "I'm not much of a baseball fan, but I do know that the Yankees are pretty good."

"Pretty good? They're going to run away with the American League."

"Really?" she said, looking him in the eye and pushing out her new breasts.

With only a little encouragement, the guy spent the next ten minutes telling her about the pennant race. "You should be glad you're a Yankees fan," the guy across the aisle said. "I'm a Mets fan and it's a sad year for us."

"There's always hope," the guy in the seat behind said.

Soon they were all chatting about baseball. *Holy cow,* she thought, *I'm in the center of a bunch of really nice guys. My wish is working!*

It seemed that during the day her breasts kept growing. Only a tiny bit at a time, but by the time she got home, she had D-cup tits. She had stopped at a store on the way home and bought three new bras and a new sweater, one more suited to her new body. Tight. Almost formfitting.

"Okay, genie," she said as she put on the sweater and a short skirt, "what do I talk to guys about?"

"You discovered that this morning," the genie said. "Don't try to learn what guys like, just ask questions. Be interested in what interests them. Encourage them to talk about themselves. That really works. Oh, and use some makeup."

In the bathroom, she rummaged in a drawer and found some liner and mascara, which she applied reasonably competently. "Lipstick and cheek color," the genie advised, and she added that, too.

All made-up and looking pretty good, if she did say so herself, she grabbed her purse and headed for Hansen's, a bar about a block from her apartment. She'd never been there before, so there was no danger of meeting someone who'd remember her flat chest. Her clothes had obscured her new figure to her coworkers, and she planned to keep it that way—office romances were too messy.

The after-work crowd was bunched at the bar, but guys made space for her. "I haven't seen you in here before," one said. "Do you live around here?" another said. "My name's Bernie." "Mine's Frank." "What are you doing later, gorgeous?"

She was overwhelmed. As the evening progressed, she narrowed the crowd down to three guys. She followed the genie's advice and asked a few questions, then listened. It worked better than she could have hoped. Guys talked with her and seemed to enjoy her company. Eventually she and a guy named Seth wandered back toward her apartment, his arm draped over her shoulder. He was just walking her home, but as they reached her building, he said, "I'd really like to come up to your place."

Should she? On a first date? She hadn't had a guy up to her apartment in, well, pretty much in forever. Seth turned her to face him and leaned forward. His lips found hers and his hand found her breast. "Mmm," he purred. "Nice mouth."

Audrey could tell that her mouth wasn't really what was attracting him to her. His hand slipped beneath her sweater and slid up her ribs. When his fingers reached her bra, he cupped her silk-covered breast and squeezed her already erect nipple. She almost swooned.

They didn't stop in her living room, but rather want directly to the bedroom. He quickly pulled her sweater off over her head, removed her bra, and buried his face in her cleavage. Fingers pinched each nipple. Her knees buckled and Seth almost had to carry her to the bed.

Quickly he dragged off his clothing, put on a condom, and slid his erect cock into her waiting body. It was heaven. He pounded into her, hands still on her breasts, mouth moving from one area of flesh to another. He thrust harder, then flipped over onto his back and settled her astride his erection. "God, I love your tits," he yelled, filling his hands with her large breasts and putting his nose between them.

She bounced and wriggled, taking all the pleasure he could give. "You feel so good," she cried as she reached down and rubbed her clit, as she did so often in bed, alone. Arching her back and stroking herself, she came and, with a roar, so did he. Limp, they both collapsed on the bed and lay there, trying to breathe.

"That was great," he said eventually as he got up and stepped into his shorts and slacks. Leaving her on the bed, he finished dressing and, saying he'd see her the following evening at Hansen's, he left.

She was totally satisfied. "Thanks, genie," she whispered as she fell asleep.

The following evening the scene was repeated, only with a man named Pete. And again the next night with Timothy.

On the fourth night of her changed life, she arrived in the apartment with a hunk named Connor. Her boobs had grown to almost mammoth proportions and she knew that Connor couldn't wait to get his hands on her. "You know," she said as her apartment door closed behind them, "I'd love to pour you a beer. Then maybe you could tell me a little about yourself."

She watched the frustration flood his face. "I'm thirty-six, divorced, no kids. I work at an insurance agency. That enough chit-chat?"

"I just thought . . ."

"Don't think," he purred, grabbing her breasts. "Just feel."

"You're doing enough feeling for both of us," she said, a nasty edge creeping into her voice.

"Your boobs are so soft. I thought they'd feel fake . . ."

"Listen, Connor," she said, fed up with guys wanting only to touch her breasts, "let's slow down a little."

He looked deeply disappointed. "Several of the guys said . . ."

They talked. Of course. She should have known that. "They talked about me?" she said to see what the conversation had been.

"Well," he hesitated. "They just said that you were such fun."

"In bed."

"Well, sure."

"Not tonight," she said, now disgusted with herself.

"Come on, honey, what's the harm? You were attracted to me in the bar. I'm good in bed and I can give you a good ride."

She slowly shook her head. "Not tonight."

"But, baby . . ."

"Honey. Baby. Okay, what's my name?"

"Uh . . ."

"Out, Connor. Now! I'm not interested."

Reluctantly, Connor left. "Genie!" she called. She hadn't seen him since that evening four nights ago when he told her about her wishes.

"Yes, Audrey. See, I remember your name."

A slow smile softened her face. "I've been a jerk, right?"

"Partly," the genie admitted. "You wanted to be popular, have guys. Good sex. I don't fault you for that. It's just that big boobs aren't the answer, as I think you've found out."

She let out a long breath. "Yeah, but it started out so well."

"Your newfound self-confidence isn't misplaced. You've had some good conversations with guys and you've learned how to talk with them."

"That was fine the first night, but since then all they are interested in is my chest and my bedroom."

"Want the chest back to the way it was?"

She grinned. "Well, a B-cup wouldn't be all bad. But the rest? Not so much."

"Now you see what you saved the third wish for. We can put your body back, with a few minor modifications, if that's what you want."

"What about talking to guys?"

"That's been all you, and my suggestions, of course," he said, buffing his nails on his shirt front. "I'm pretty good with socializing."

She thought back on the past week. He was right. She'd spent some quality time with a few people at the office and one or two at Hansen's. But the tits had to go. "I wish . . ."

"Got it. Spending the third wish," the genie said, and her breasts slowly deflated to a lovely, soft B-cup, which went well with the few curves he'd left her.

In the bedroom, she checked the mirror and smiled. She liked what she saw. "Thanks, genie, for the education."

"Unintended consequences. You just never know. Now you might want to donate my bottle back to Goodwill so someone else can get wishes."

"Right you are. But if you don't mind, I'll keep you on my shelf for a little while to remind me of everything. I hate to think of you all cramped up in that bottle, though."

"I don't really mind. However, if you could give me something soft to cuddle with, that would help."

Laughing, she strode into her bedroom, opened her lingerie drawer and pulled out one of her size-D bras, a particularly satiny one she'd never worn. A pair of scissors made short work of detaching one of the cups.

In the living room, she handed the bit of silky fabric to the genie. "Fabulous," he purred.

Still stroking his cheek with the cloth, slowly, the genie became smoke and the smoke curled back into the bottle and she put it in the shadow box beside the ruby vase. "Thanks, genie," she whispered, "for everything."

Good Hands

Okay, I'll fess up. Occasionally I go to a massage parlor. I do get a massage, of course, but it's always followed by some hanky-panky. I'm a pretty attractive guy, but I love the no-fuss idea of paying for services rendered. No hassle, no worries about who calls whom the following week. I just pay for it and get my rocks off.

Several weeks ago I wanted a slow, drawn-out orgasm, just the thing that Good Hands can give me. Good Hands is a massage parlor that gives real folks real massages, by licensed massage therapists. It also gives special services if you know how to ask. Of course, by now they know me and know what I want. That evening they suggested a very special kind of massage. The booking lady gave it an Asian name, but she explained it involved being massaged by two women.

As she talked my cock got hard. Two women, four hands, a dream come true. Pay extra? Sure. Why not? Book 'em, Danno.

After she swiped my credit card, she directed me to suite seven. It was always a suite. The term might be a little upmarket, but the rooms were, in fact, lovely. They all had the de rigueur leather-covered massage table with the special headrest with the opening in the middle so that when you're facedown you don't mash your nose. Pictures hung on the walls. Some were watercolor landscapes; some were deeply erotic scenes of sex in every conceivable position. There was usually an overstuffed sofa and several lamps that cast a pastel glow, and most rooms also had candles that could be lit to increase the ambiance. Got that? *Ambiance.* Upscale word for an upscale place.

I'd been in suite seven before so I wasn't surprised by the living-room atmosphere, except for the fornication photos on the walls, that is. It also had several large mirrors on the walls and the ceiling was mirrored as well. Classical music played quietly in the background. It was very warm in the room, and I wanted to quickly remove my clothes, but I waited. The masseuse usually removed my clothing, very slowly, touching and stroking each part as she uncovered it.

I waited for no more than a minute, then two women walked in. I guess many men want gorgeous women in their early twenties with long blond hair and silicone breasts. Me, I want women who know their way around, if you get my drift. Maybe closer to my age, women who haven't giggled in many years. I'd been with Maryanne before and she smiled. "Welcome, Don." She's maybe thirty, with a relatively pretty face, the bluest eyes, and a great, welcoming smile. She had on a short, lightweight robe that showed off her long legs. She indicated the woman standing beside her. "This is Gloria."

Gloria was a little younger than Maryanne, maybe late twenties, with short, curly red hair, green eyes, and the most beautiful hands, long fingers with bright red nails. "Nice to meet you, Don," she said, her voice soft and melodious.

I really love this place.

"Now," Maryanne said, "let's get you undressed."

Having two women fussing over you is something not to be missed. I closed my eyes, not caring who did what. I wanted to concentrate on the feeling of four hands working on my belt, my sneaker laces, my shirt buttons. The brush of soft fingertips over my chest, my calves, my back was heavenly.

I heard soft, feminine purring. "Umm." They liked what they saw as they stripped me. They liked my body. I try to keep myself in good shape, but of course, they're paid to like my body. Forget that. I liked the illusion.

I was hard as a rock and my rigid cock stuck out from my groin, but they ignored that part of me and that was fine. I was in no hurry.

"Okay, Don," Maryanne said. "Lie on your stomach."

As I opened my eyes, I watched Gloria spread a large, fluffy towel on the table and she helped me onto it. I adjusted my softening erection beneath my pubic bone. "Now, just close your eyes again," she said. "Feel. Feel everything."

They started with my legs. They coordinated their movements so their oily hands were synchronized, in unison, one woman working on each leg, stroking, kneading. Until I began getting massages at Good Hands, I had never realized how sensitive my skin was, nor had I ever taken the time to figure it out. Maryanne and her compatriots showed me.

Occasionally fingers worked on the inside of my thighs, close to my balls, but they never quite touched me there, although I'm sure they knew I ached for it. They were experts at how to keep me on the edge. Fabulous.

Then they moved to my feet, sliding slick fingers between my toes, and pulling on each as though they were pulling on my cock. Two sets of hands, four thumbs pressing into my arches. Shit, I was in heaven.

Maryanne and Gloria moved to my back and shoulders, still totally in sync. One pair of hands on my left side, one set on my right.

My arms came next. They played with my fingers, brushing their erect nipples over the backs of my hands.

Eventually Maryanne said, "Time to turn over," and I did. At first I was a little embarrassed by my erection, but that's totally silly. We all know that this is what the hour is all about.

"You didn't tell me he was so well endowed," I heard Gloria say.

"I thought I'd leave that for a surprise," Maryanne replied. Lies? Do they say that to every guy? Probably, but it sure made me feel great.

Again they started with my legs but they spent much less time there. Their attention to my arms was brief as well, but my hands got special treatment. Each woman bent over and filled my palm with a breast, rubbing their nipples against my skin. They moved on to my face, again using oily breast flesh to caress my skin. "Open," Maryanne said, nipples gliding over my lips. She certainly does know what I like.

I opened my mouth and felt two erect nipples enter my mouth. "Suck."

I did. I'd never sucked on two women's nipples at the same time. I was blissful. I cupped the two breasts and stroked the flesh as I sucked. Eventually they pulled back. I heard a hum as the table lowered. They extended my arms and each woman straddled a hand. Wet pussies, one in each hand. I fingered the folds, then slowly slipped a finger into each sopping cunt.

Hands found my cock then, again perfectly synchronized, and began fondling my penis and balls. Tongues licked up each side while fingers played with the crack in my ass. Hot breath wafted over my wet erection as my fingers worked. Then I pulled my hands back and grabbed Gloria by the hips. The table was low enough that she could straddle my face while Maryanne climbed onto my now-condom-covered cock. The room filled with the sounds of heavy panting and low moans, the air reeked of sex.

The combination of my mouth filled with pussy and a pussy surrounding my cock was too much. I came and I suspected, hoped, that Gloria and Maryanne did, too. Am I flattering myself? Who cares?

We all rested, then the women washed me with warm, wet cloths, and helped me dress.

"Come back soon," Maryanne said.

"And if you enjoyed the evening, ask for us both again," Gloria added.

I was so totally sated that I could barely stand. "You bet I will."

An Adventure in Poland

My husband, Tony, and I recently took a driving trip through Eastern Europe. We'd been married for about six months so this was actually a honeymoon of sorts. It was a great trip: zillions of places to see and things to do. And lots of newly married sex. But the trip itself isn't the point of my story.

It all began while we were driving through Poland, near the Slovakian border. Suddenly Tony slowed the car and asked me to close my eyes. He told me he wanted to buy a surprise for me and didn't want me to peek. He had that hot, sexy look he gets sometimes, and, since I know he's got a deliciously devious mind, I did as he asked.

He pulled the car over and I squeezed my eyes shut and heard him get out. We don't speak any Polish, but I guess he made himself understood since a few minutes later he popped open the trunk on our little rental car, fussed around for a while, then put something inside. "Don't open yet," he yelled from the back of the car.

"I won't," I promised and eventually we drove away.

"Okay, you can open your eyes now."

I couldn't imagine what he could have bought from a store or roadside stand in rural Poland, and for several minutes I racked my brain. I came up empty. Tony comes up with such wonderful ideas that I was getting impatient.

"Be patient, love, and you'll be rewarded. I promise."

My panties moistened at the mere thought of what he might have in mind.

When we got back to our hotel, he removed a large canvas tote bag we had with us and, hugging it to his chest, walked beside me to our room, where he stashed the bag in the armoire.

Throughout dinner I couldn't keep my mind from whatever it was that Tony had stashed in the closet.

We finished dessert but, rather than seek out the local night life, we returned to our room. "Okay, Tony, what's the surprise?"

"Still impatient, aren't you?"

"You know me well enough to know that I am. Give!"

"In good time. First, take off all your clothes."

Never one to argue with my husband when he's in one of those moods, I quickly stripped.

"Okay, hold out your arms." I stretched out my arms in front of me and Tony quickly fastened my wrists together using part of a roll of gauze from the first-aid kit we carry for emergencies. "That's to keep you from doing anything with those talented fingers of yours except what I tell you." We'd played light bondage games before, but not often. Tony's usually not one for mastery, but tonight he was setting the rules.

"Yes, sir," I said, a slightly military tone in my voice. There's little subservience in me, but we could both count on the fact that I wouldn't spoil his, or my, fun.

"Now turn around." I heard him tearing something, then, from behind me, he placed a pad over each eye and used the rest of the roll of gauze to tie a blindfold over them. "This will take a moment so just stand there until I'm ready."

My breath had thickened and my crotch was already twitchy. "What's going on, Tony? I'm dying of curiosity."

"Too bad, Janet. You'll just have to wait."

"*Wait.* There's that word again."

"Yup. Tonight is going to be a lesson in patience."

I chuckled. My sexual impatience has become a running joke between us. As he pounds into me and I scream, "Do it, do it, do it," he often says, "Some day I'm going to have to teach you to delay gratification."

As I stood, naked, in the middle of our hotel room, I heard lots of moving around. Finally he guided me to the edge of the bed. "Okay, lie down. I'll help." I stretched out on the bed and Tony deftly flipped me over onto my stomach, extending my tied wrists over my head. Beneath my naked body I felt something wonderfully soft and furry. "Wriggle around and feel that," he said.

I was lying on the most sensual thing I think I'd ever felt. My breasts were being caressed by the softest fur. "What is this?"

"I saw a stand selling large, real fur pelts and I couldn't resist. They tried to tell me what they were but I didn't really understand, but they were so soft and beautiful that I couldn't resist. And they weren't even expensive." As I moved against the fur, I felt another pelt being brushed over my buttocks. "I bought two."

"My God," I said, getting wet immediately. "That's the most erotic thing I've ever felt."

"I thought as much." Then he began to slowly stroke me, my calves, arms, shoulders, and backs of my upper thighs and buttocks. When he used a corner of the furry cloth to caress the insides of my thighs I thought I'd gone to sensual heaven. "Nice?"

I could only purr.

"Turn over, but keep your hands over your head. I wouldn't want those fingers wandering."

I knew exactly what he meant. Masturbation played a part in some of our games, but he didn't want me to satisfy my hunger, much as I wanted to.

Then he began to tease me in earnest. The fur briefly brushed against one nipple, then moved to one elbow. He stroked it lightly between my legs, then across my lips. Since I was still blindfolded, I couldn't figure out where he would caress next and the surprise was totally erotic.

Suddenly something different rubbed against my lips. I have no idea when he removed his clothing, but his naked cock now stroked my mouth. "Open," he said.

I did as he asked and found my lips and tongue being caressed by his member while the fur rubbed my breasts. "Mmm," I moaned, flying off into space.

Then I felt the fur against my face. Tony was obviously rubbing both of us while he fucked my mouth. "You are irresistible," he said, his voice hoarse, his breathing ragged. He began to fuck my mouth more forcefully, his free hand tangled in the hair on the back of my head. I love the feel of him in my mouth and I caressed him with my tongue. I wanted to reach out and scratch his balls the way he likes, but my hands were still tied and stretched above my head.

He came quickly, and I swallowed his semen.

As I panted I felt him spread my legs and climb between. When his mouth found my slit and the fur rubbed my belly

I started climbing. Let me tell you, he knows exactly how to flick his tongue over my clit, finding just the right rhythm. "Yes," I moaned, as I rose higher and higher. "Don't stop. Do it, do it, do it."

Then he backed off, moving to my arms and untying my wrists. "Still no patience. You want it? Well, you'll just have to do it yourself while I watch." Then he slipped off the blindfold. "And I want you to know I'm watching, so don't close your eyes."

I fastened my gaze on his eyes while I slid my fingers through my soaked folds. He leaned forward and breathed hot air on the skin of my groin and I found my clit and rubbed. "Yes, baby," he said, "show me. Take what you want, what you need."

And I did.

"Tell me when you come. I want to know."

"God, yes. Put your finger inside me so you can feel it."

And he did.

I came, pulses, waves of pleasure rocketing through me. My hips bucked. "Yes, yes, yes," I said as my orgasm overwhelmed me.

Later, when we'd caught our breath, he said, "I thought you'd like those pelts."

"I'm afraid one's pretty wet."

"We have another."

I giggled. "Yes, we do. Next time you get to lie on it and I get to play."

Her Final Assignment

SHE WORE A DIAPHANOUS GOWN, JUST AS HE HAD DREAMED her for the past several nights. His nymph. Okay, enough. This was just another dream. It must be that simple. Right? Yet she stood at the foot of his bed, gorgeous raven hair drifting down her back, her caramel-colored nipples and dark pubic hair faintly visible beneath the gown. She sure looked real, more real than ever before. *But what is a nymph doing in my bedroom?* Walt wondered.

"You wanted me here, so here I am," she said, her voice like music.

"Excuse me?"

"You called me here and so . . ."

"I called you?" He was barely coherent.

"You've been calling for me for almost a week. You've summoned me as surely as if you had yelled my name."

"Your name?" He was aware that he sounded like an ass, but he had no idea how she had gotten into his room. His mind was totally befuddled. *Okay, Walt, think. You went out with the guys, had a few too many beers, went home, and collapsed on the bed. I've got that.* He glanced at the clock beside his bed—3:07. He'd gone to sleep, okay, passed out, at about one, so he'd been asleep for a couple of hours. Maybe he was still asleep. That was it, he was asleep, dreaming.

"No, you're not asleep," she said in that wonderfully mellifluous voice. "I'm really here, and you have but to command me."

"Right, now I get it. Rog or Tony. Right? They put you up to this. Paid you for a joke."

"No, they didn't bring me here. You did. However, if it makes you feel better to believe that, fine. I'm still yours to command."

"Right again." His voice was not stingingly sarcastic. "Okay, you've got a hidden camera. The joke's on me."

She shook her head slowly. "You know, you're too suspicious. You have to learn to live a bit."

Walt sat up and ran his fingers through his hair. "Sorry, hon. A joke's a joke and I'm done with this one."

Still shaking her head she said, "All right, I can take a hint. I'll go."

"Hint? It's a downright demand. I'm not in the mood for the guys' pranks."

"Done. However, let's make a deal. I'll leave and come back when you've accepted me and what I am."

He looked her over. Under any other circumstances he'd be more than happy to give her the run of his anatomy, but he had a headache and just wasn't up to his pals' pranks. "Good. You do that."

Poof. She disappeared. She didn't walk out of the room, she sort of winked out. His mouth fell open. No real person blinked out of existence. *Poof.* Like that. Damn. It looked as if he'd just passed up the offer of a lifetime. "Holy shit," he said under his breath. "Okay, I believe. I believe. Come back."

Poof. She was back.

"How? Why? What?" he stammered.

"That's better. I was beginning to think you weren't going to be reasonable about this. I have my orders and you're it."

"I repeat. How and why?"

"The how? I have no clue. The big boss seems to know when someone's been making a big enough wish and so he assigned one of us to be with you for one night."

"One night? Tonight?"

"Yes." She was starting to sound a little exasperated. "You are so full of questions, none of them the right ones."

"Like which right ones?"

"Like what can we do together? I'm an expert in good old hot sex, fellatio, and anal play. I can paddle you if you're into that stuff, or you can spank me. I'm fully trained in all kinds of sex acts. I've been doing this for a long time. If the truth were known, so long that you're my last assignment. Then I'm . . . Well, I don't know exactly where I'll go from here, but I've got a few ideas. Anyway, this is my swan song, so to speak."

"Fellatio? Anal sex?" God, he was really sounding like a fool but he was so flummoxed that he couldn't get his brain to make sense of all this.

She glided toward the bed, sat on the edge, and put one hand on his bare chest pushing him onto his back. He stared at her slender fingers with their long, deep red nails. Slowly she scratched her way across his nipples. "Getting the idea?" she purred.

How had she known how sensitive his nipples were? He closed his eyes. "Umm," he groaned. "That feels nice."

"Of course it does."

"You know, I might just roll with this. Who cares whether the guys are pulling a fast one on me?" In case there was a hidden camera, he waved weakly in the air. "Okay, guys. I'm good with this."

"Great. Let's get to it." There was an edge to her voice. "Just lie back and enjoy it, and if you've got any suggestions, let me know." Her grin was wide, but seemed false. She seemed almost angry. At him?

He opened his eyes. "You're beginning to sound like my ex-girlfriend. You know, a bit of an attitude."

She looked at him, her face all innocent, her smile now

syrupy. "Not at all," she said, almost pulling off the act. "I have no idea what you're talking about."

He moved back on the bed and sat up with his back against the headboard. "Sure you do. Come on, give. What's up, really?"

She sat back on her haunches, looked him in the eye, then softened and sighed. "You're right. I'm being a bit cranky. This is my last job. Forever. I guess I just want to get on with everything."

"Job. Explain what this is all about. I know you're no ordinary hooker. Hookers don't appear and disappear the way you do."

With another long sigh, she stood and paced beside the bed. "Well, you see it's like this: We nymphs are required to satisfy a certain number of humans before we can move on to more adventurous things."

"Adventurous?"

"You guys are so predictable. You want either hand jobs or oral. Occasionally anal but that's infrequent. I'm trained for all kinds of kinky fun, but no, not for earth guys. Sucking and fucking and that's about it. It's like porn movies. Come shots. That's all guys can think of. So we do what you want, regardless of whether it's good for us or not. You're the final fuck of my quota"—she stood beside the bed—"so let's just do this. Cunt or mouth?"

"Not so fast." He patted the bed beside his hip and she sat. "You mean no one asks what you want?"

"Oh, pleeeeezzze. Be real. Not one person. You get a nymph, get your rocks off, and *poof*, I'm gone until my next assignment." She grinned. "Now—no more 'next assignment.' Just me and fun from now on."

Walt took a moment to gather his thoughts. He was in a unique situation and he was determined to make the most of it. "Let's back up a bit. What's your name?"

She smiled her most sincere smile. "What would you like it to be?"

"Cut the bullshit. That's a hooker line. What's your real name?"

"Amanda," she said softly, dropping her chin. "Mandy."

"Well, Mandy, if I were your nymph—can there be male nymphs?"

"I suppose," she answered quietly.

"Okay. If I were your nymph, what would you want?"

"I would want whatever you wanted."

"Cut the crap." Walt sighed. "I asked you an honest question. You're here for the night so let's see what we can figure out. What would you want?"

"Hmm." She tilted her head to one side and struck a sexy pose, the tip of her index finger in her mouth. "You know I never thought about it."

Walt almost laughed. That was a pose he'd never found sexy. "More bullshit. Give!"

She let out a long breath and, seeming resigned, slowly closed her eyes. "I'd wish for someone to do it all just for me for once. I love kissing and having my breasts played with. I love receiving oral sex. I love it slow and sexy." Her eyes flashed open. "But I'm here for you. I don't think the boss would like me revealing all this stuff."

"Forget the boss. This is your last assignment so let's make the most of it." He moved off the bed and then patted the spot he'd just vacated. "Lie here." When she hesitated, he said, "You have to do what I want, right?"

She nodded, then reluctantly stretched out on the bed. He lay beside her and kissed her, played with her mouth, nibbled on her lips. "Mmm, you taste wonderful."

Her eyes closed, then snapped open. "I don't think . . ."

"Don't think, just feel." He kissed her again and realized that he was enjoying pleasing her. He heard the moans she made and felt her hips move.

He moved to her breast, sucking her erect nipple through the thin fabric of her dress. He blew on the wet spot and watched her tit contract. Then he repeated the action with her other one. "That feels really good, but . . ."

"No buts," he said. "This is what I want, so relax and just feel." He alternated between nipples until she was writhing. After he pulled her gown off, he spread her legs and crawled between. She was so wet that he could smell her arousal, all hot and sexy. Using his thumbs he parted her pussy lips and slid one finger through her folds. She was sopping, juices soaking her flesh. He was amazed. He never thought he was particularly good in bed, but he had obviously given this experienced nymph so much pleasure that she could barely hold still.

He pressed on her hip bones with his palms to hold her in place, then lowered his mouth to her cunt. When he flicked his tongue over her hard clit she groaned, and it became even more difficult to keep her body still. Then he slid his tongue over her flesh and pushed the tip into her opening.

Her clit was demanding attention so he sucked at it. "Oh, oh, oh," she said, then made a long, low moan.

He thought she tasted like honey and kept sucking. "I'm going to—come if you keep—doing that," she said, her voice hoarse, her breathing so rapid she could barely get the words out.

"Good. That's exactly what I want."

"But . . ." He sucked more forcefully and slipped his fingers back so he stroked her anus. She came then, screaming, twisting on the bed, unable to get enough of the pleasures of her orgasm.

He could barely hold her still enough to keep his mouth on her. He kept sucking and rubbing her rear opening until she lightly pushed him away. "Enough," she said, breathless. "I can't—take—any more."

Walt hadn't climaxed but he was content. He cuddled beside her and they dozed.

Later she said, "It's never been like that for me."

"I'm glad," he said, a silly grin on his face. "It was great for me, too."

"But . . ."

"You said we had the entire night so we can do more later, right?"

"Right," she said, her smile lighting up the room.

"What then? I mean after your last assignment."

"I get to choose where and what and how for myself."

He held her tightly. "That's wonderful. When you leave I will wish you well, but I'd love you to stay for a while."

She looked at him and raised an eyebrow. "I could stick around for a while. Get a job, maybe. Sort of be your girlfriend."

"You could?" he said, eyes widening. "I thought you'd, well, you know, sit on a cloud, play the harp, something like that."

"That sounds deadly dull. I'd rather be here."

Walt's grin widened still more. "I'd like that." He thought a minute. "You said you were trained in the arts of sex. Could we play with different stuff? Act out some scenarios? For both of us, I mean."

"I'd love that," she said, moving close and kissing him. "I surely would."

Teach Me

❧

ⱧOHANNA AND HER HUSBAND, RICK, LOVE TO PLAY SEX
games and occasionally discuss fantasies. Recently Rick con-
fided his deepest, darkest secret. They both knew that he
would never act on it, but occasionally, when he needed that
little final boost while they were making love, he explained
that he'd use it to push him over the edge.

Knowing his secret, Johanna had acted on it a few weeks
before. He'd been rubbing his cock while she watched. In a
small, almost babyish voice, she'd said, "Would you teach me
how to do that?" He'd come explosively.

"Would you really like to teach a teenage girl about sex?"
she had asked later as they caught their breath.

"Of course not," Rick had snapped. "I'd never touch

anyone like that for several reasons. First, I'd never do anything with anyone underage. Second, I'd never cheat on you. You should know that."

She stroked his naked chest. "Of course I know that, darling. I'm really sorry. I guess I didn't phrase that quite right. I was just wondering about the power of your fantasy."

"Fantasies don't have to be things you'd actually do," he said, totally serious. "Don't you have any lurking in the back of your mind?"

"I'd rather not talk about them. They might lose their potency."

"So you have?"

Johanna huffed out a breath. "Yes," she admitted. "Maybe I'll tell you sometime."

"I told you mine . . ."

"I know. Maybe another time."

So now, after a little preparation, she was ready to try acting out Rick's desire. She knew a little about teens and was sure that they didn't dress much differently than she did, but she thought she understood the picture Rick had formed in his mind. She'd gone to Walmart and bought some tiny, teeny-bopper undies and a matching bra that barely contained her large breasts, both hot pink with black polka dots. She'd also found a blue-and-green plaid skirt at a garage sale and added a plain white blouse. With the addition of white knee-high socks and black loafers, she looked enough like a high school girl that she was sure Rick's mind could do the rest.

That afternoon she'd gotten home from work early and dressed up. She was just finishing when she heard, "I'm home."

She said nothing, just walked from the bedroom to the living room. "Hello," she said softly.

Rick's eyes widened and he stared silently. A few times before, she'd greeted him in some outfit or other, once a nurse, once a cop, and once wearing nothing but a raincoat, a bra, a garter belt, and what she called her whorehouse shoes, four-inch silver spikes. He was quick on the uptake, and he always got into the game quickly. Role playing led to great sex. Tonight, however, he was mute.

Had she gone too far? She had penetrated one of his most secret places. Would he feel that she was invading? She was having serious second thoughts, but she decided to push just a little further. If he seemed too uncomfortable, she'd back off. "I was babysitting down the block but as I passed your house I needed to use the bathroom. I hope you don't mind."

She hadn't erred. Rick's eyes never left her as he breathed heavily. He managed to say, "Not at all. No. I don't mind at all."

Johanna's mouth widened into a smile. "That's good. I'm glad." She meant that on many levels. When Rick didn't pick up the conversation, she continued, "I've seen you around, you know."

"You have?"

"Sure. Sometimes, when you mow the lawn without your

shirt, I watch you. You're quite a hunk." Johanna had to agree with her alter ego. Rick was indeed quite a hunk.

"W-w-what's your name?"

She watched him take a deep breath, hands trembling. He was totally flummoxed and, from the tent in the front of his slacks, also very aroused. "Mary," Johanna said, saying the first name that came into her mind. "And I know yours is Rick." He became silent again so she said, "How about we sit on the sofa for a few minutes? I don't have to be home for a while." After a pause, she said, "I could tell you about school."

She watched Rick take another long, shuddering breath and let it out slowly. "I would like to hear about your school," he said.

They sat on the couch and she made up stories about her imaginary school, teachers, and friends. Finally she said, "All my girlfriends have boyfriends, but I don't. It's pretty lame." *Lame. Good word*, she thought.

During their discussion, Rick had loosened up and relaxed enough to truly get into the scenario. "I can't imagine why not. You're pretty and smart."

Johanna beamed. "You really think so? That I'm pretty, I mean?"

"Oh, most certainly."

Johanna sighed. "But I don't know how to kiss boys, and they know it. I think that's why no one will ask me out. They think I'm a dork when it comes to sex. I do know stuff.

I've read stuff. I watch talk shows. But I've . . . well, I've never . . ."

"That doesn't matter. Boys will like you for what you are. However, I could show you a few things, just to give you a start."

Her face lit. Giving him her most enthusiastic grin, she said, "Would you? Really? Would you?"

Rick's smile was wide and genuine. This was his fantasy and he'd obviously gotten deeply into it. "Sure. I could help out."

It was all Johanna could do not to cheer. This was working out better than she'd ever expected. She was actually enjoying the prospect of Rick teaching her about sex. "Now? Right now?"

Rick curled his index finger and used the knuckle to lift her chin. "Okay, let's start here." He brushed his lips over hers, lightly, barely touching the surface. Over and over he teased her mouth, until she heard her heart pounding in her ears. His tongue flicked over the joining of her lips. "Now open for me."

His mouth pressed against hers and she parted her lips slightly. He cupped the back of her head and held it so he could adjust the position of their kiss. She loved kissing but they didn't usually spend much time on it, both being eager to get to the serious stuff. Now they spent long minutes just enjoying each other's mouths. Tongues dueling, she placed her hands on his chest, then slipped one to the back of his neck.

When they parted, both panting, in the persona of Mary, she said, "Was that okay?"

"My God," he said, barely able to get two words out. "Okay?" He took a few deep breaths. "If it were any better . . ."

"Could you show me more?" she said, lowering her gaze and making her voice little. She didn't have to simulate her trembling.

"I think that could be arranged," he said, reaching over and unfastening the top button of her shirt. As her tiny spotted bra was revealed, he smiled and said, "That's very pretty."

She dropped her head even farther until her chin was almost pressed against her chest. In a tiny voice she said, "I bought it for you."

"You had this planned?" he said, and Johanna wasn't sure whether he was talking to her or to Mary. But she remained Mary and spoke as she thought a naive teen would.

"Yes." Her voice was almost inaudible. "I hope that's okay."

"I'm glad you did," he said, running his fingertip over the satiny bra cup. "It's very lovely."

"It's got matching panties," she blurted out.

"I think I'll get to see those later." By that time he had all the buttons open and the tails of the blouse pulled from the skirt. He slipped the top down her arms and tossed it away. "Lovely," he said, extending his hands and brushing the tips of her still-covered breasts with his palms. As he lightly swirled his fingertips over her breasts, he leaned forward and touched his lips to hers. Her sigh was long and deep, her excitement making her entire body tremble. The lengthy foreplay and expectations were making her incredibly hot.

Eventually, when she could wait no longer, she slipped her hands up Rick's chest and placed one hand on either side of his cheeks as they kissed.

"You seem to know about kissing, Mary," Rick said.

"I hope it pleases you," she whispered.

"Oh, it does. But now I want to see what this lovely pink satin covers. Can I remove it?"

"Yes. Of course. What should I do?"

"Nothing yet. I'll teach you what you need to know. Right now, just enjoy what I'm doing." He unhooked the bra and allowed Johanna's large breasts to fall free. She'd gotten into the fantasy enough that it felt like he was seeing her for the first time. It made her surprisingly hungry for him.

"Wonderful," he purred, grazing her flesh with his fingertips.

"May I feel you, too?" she asked.

"Mmmm," he answered, so she slowly unbuttoned his shirt and removed it. Then, as he had done, she stroked his bare chest with her palms and watched his nipples harden. After more than a year of marriage, she'd not been aware that he had sensitive nipples. She'd have to remember that.

"What should I do now?" she asked, wanting to move more quickly.

"Would you take off your skirt for me?"

"Oh, yes," she said, standing and slowly unfastening the zipper, letting the plaid slide to the floor. She wiggled her hips. "See the matching panties?"

"I see, and I like what they cover. Will you take them off for me, too?"

Slowly, as if stripping in a club, she pulled her panties off, removing her shoes and socks at the same time. "Should I undress you, too?"

"I'd like that," he said, so when he stood, she unfastened his belt and slacks and let everything fall. It was very obvious that he was aroused.

"Ohhh," she said, palming his erection, "you're very big. I don't know whether . . ."

"Don't worry about anything, Mary," he said, chuckling. "Everything will work."

"What should I do now?"

"If you take my shorts off you can touch me, if you'd like."

"I would like that."

She pulled off his shorts and stared as his engorged cock. "May I touch it? I don't want to hurt you."

"You won't and I'd love it if you'd touch me."

So she did. "Like this?" she asked, making awkward stroking motions with only the pads of her fingers.

He grabbed her wrist and curled her fingers around

his cock. "Like this," he said, growing impatient. She surrounded him with her hand and he bucked his hips, fucking her fist. "God, you're making me crazy," he said. "Let's go to the bedroom where we can be more comfortable."

Still holding his erection she walked beside him, down the hall and into the bedroom. Hands on her shoulders, he pushed her until she was sitting on the edge of the bed. He stepped between her knees and cupped her face. "Will you take me into your mouth?"

She parted her lips and licked the tip of his dripping cock. "Show me how."

"I'm sure you don't need any training. Just do what feels good."

Johanna had always enjoyed giving her husband head and this time was no different. She licked the length of him. "I'm pretending that you're a Dum Dum Pop." She hesitated. "But you taste even better."

His chuckle was deep and hoarse. "I would like it if you'd suck it."

She opened her mouth and closed her lips around his staff. She created a vacuum and pulled him inside, then drew back maintaining the suction, just the way he liked it. When his cock emerged, she said, "You mean like this?"

"Just like that."

After just a few strokes, he could obviously hold back no longer. He pushed her onto her back and rammed his cock into her, fucking her like a crazed man until, with only a few thrusts, he came. Although she hadn't climaxed she was in heaven. Rick was so obviously happy that she knew they'd repeat the game from time to time. And next time she'd let him teach her about the way a woman likes to receive oral sex.

Potions

HE STORE WAS REALLY NARROW WITH A FRONT WINDOW
so grimy that Dale couldn't see inside. POTIONS, in tattered
gold lettering, was all that was written on the window. That
and, in tiny print at the bottom, P. DEARLY, PROP.

Potions. That was an odd name for a store. Was that its
name or the product it sold? And why hadn't he noticed this
disreputable excuse for a store before? After all, it was right
on his way home from the supermarket. He shifted his bag
of groceries from one hip to the other and considered going
inside. Potions for what? The common cold? Athlete's foot?
Beauty products? Yeah, that was probably it. Beauty stuff.

He was about to continue toward his house, then he
stopped himself. He was curious, so he opened the heavy door

and went inside. As he entered, a cheery little bell announced his arrival. To no one. No customers. No P. Dearly, Prop.

The place was as dingy inside as the outside would indicate. Dusty shelves filled with bottles, vials, and jugs, small boxes and odd-shaped containers in all colors and shapes. Well, they had originally been many different colors but most were so dirty and covered with stains that he couldn't make out the original hue.

"Good afternoon, young man. I'm Mr. Dearly." A wizened, stooped old man appeared through a curtain that led, Dale thought, to the back of the store. The man wore grungy black pants and a black vest better suited for the ragbag, over a grayish shirt, its original color indistinguishable. His voice sounded not unlike a squeaking door.

"Good afternoon." Dearly? What an odd name for a truly odd-looking man in an odd-feeling store.

"Welcome," the man's voice creaked. "Feel free to look around."

"At what? I have no idea what you sell in here."

"I sell potions of all kinds. What did you have in mind?"

"I don't know," Dale said. "Give me some suggestions of what you have."

"We have potions to cure what ails you, to fix what needs fixing, to give you courage, strength, sexual potency, like that."

Dale fastened on to the phrase *sexual potency*. "You mean like those ads in magazines or the ones on television?"

"Not quite. Those things are, for the most part, rip-offs. My potions work."

Dale thought about sexual potency. That wouldn't do him any good unless he had a girlfriend to use it with. His sigh was heartfelt. He thought about himself, slightly nerdy, with glasses that were forever slipping down his nose, nondescript, mousy brown hair, and ordinary looks. He met his share of women in clubs, bars, and at work, but no one ever gave him much of a second look. He glanced around the shop, then shifted his bag to his other hip and started to turn.

"Don't leave yet," the little man said. "There must be something you would wish for."

"Wish for? Unfortunately you haven't got anything to cure what ails me."

Mr. Dearly looked him over for a moment. "I have a potion to help you with women."

"Enough," Dale said. "You look me over and figure I'm a loser just like that." He snapped his fingers and started for the door.

"Don't dismiss my irresistibility potion so quickly."

"Irresistibility potion? You've got to be kidding." He had to admit he was intrigued, however.

"Not at all, young man. It really works." He shuffled to a bookcase and removed a bottle, only slightly less grimy than the rest. "This is a very popular seller. A few drops of this behind your ears and the women won't be able to leave you alone."

Hand on the door handle, he said, "Right. I don't believe a word of it."

"First vial is free. If you don't like it, don't buy more."

Dale turned. "Free?" Who was he to pass up free stuff?

"That's right, free." At the counter, Mr. Dearly decanted a minuscule amount of the liquid from the bottle into a tiny tube, then sealed it with a tiny cork. "This amount is good for one day. Try it and see what happens."

"Free? Really?"

"Really. Like so many other companies, I make my money on the reorders."

"Well . . ." What did he have to lose? He didn't have to drink the stuff, so the guy wasn't dispensing addictive drugs. What the hell? "Okay. I'll try it."

With the tiny tube in his shirt pocket, he went home.

That evening he was meeting a few male friends for dinner at a nearby restaurant. Before setting out he opened the vial and sniffed. No odor. How could anything without an aroma do anything? *Oh well*, he thought as he dabbed a little of the liquid behind each ear, emptying the vial. Still no smell.

Since they went to this place often, he and his friends gathered at their usual booth in the back. By the time the waitress came to take their order Dale had forgotten about the potion.

"Hi, guys," Sharon, their usual waitress, said. Then she

stared at Dale and, pad in hand, plunked herself down on his lap. She stared into his eyes. "What would everyone like? What would *you* like, sugar?" she asked in her sexy Southern accent.

He was speechless. Nothing like this had ever . . . She'd never shown any interest in anyone, and they'd all tried. Sharon was gorgeous, with a long auburn ponytail, huge blue eyes, and gigantic boobs. Accidentally or on purpose she brushed her breasts against his chest.

The three other guys at the table were equally flabbergasted. There was a long silence, then Sharon said, still staring at him, "I get off at ten. Meet me out back?"

"Sure." *Holy shit! Holy shit!!!*

She stood and eventually everyone ordered beers, burgers, and fries.

"What the hell was that all about?" Steve asked.

"You won the lottery and she knows it. That must be it," Mickey chimed in.

Dale remained silent, unwilling to discuss the irresistibility potion. That was the reason for this, right? The proprietor of the store couldn't have set this up. How would he know that the guys were going to meet here? He just shrugged and changed the subject.

A few moments later Sharon returned, doled out steins of beer from her tray, then dropped onto his lap again. Rubbing her big boobs against him, she planted a deep kiss on his lips, then left. The same thing occurred moments later when she brought their dinners. There was no conversation at the table until she was gone.

"What's going on?" Mickey asked again.

"I have no clue," he said, then smiled, not responding to any more of his friends' comments. Eventually the third degree faded when the football game came on the TV over the bar and the conversation moved onto other topics.

Sharon stayed away from the table and a male server finished with them. After they paid the check, the four stood on the sidewalk outside before separating. "You gonna meet her?" Steve asked.

With a wide grin, Dale said, "Of course."

"You'll have to give us all the details tomorrow."

Grin still on his face, Dale said, "I never kiss and tell."

"Bullshit," all three said in unison.

When Sharon emerged from the back door of the restaurant at exactly ten, Dale was waiting. Without a word she walked up to him, draped her arms around his neck, and french-kissed him, tongue probing deep into his mouth. He could barely breathe.

Her hands were all over him, finally settling on his groin, deftly massaging his hard cock through his pants. Finally, breathless, she said, "My car's over there."

He lived only a few blocks away but if she wanted to drive . . .

She didn't. She opened the back door and all but dragged him inside. Unzipping his fly, she bent down and took him deep into her throat, licking and sucking until he was hard as stone. When she straddled him, poised above his dick, he quickly realized that she wore nothing under the skirt of her waitress uniform—she'd taken off her panties before coming out.

That was his last coherent thought. His dick was so hard it was almost painful and he was afraid he'd shoot his load before they'd gotten started. Fortunately he didn't have to wait long. She quickly lowered her sopping pussy onto his hard-on and, bouncing, screaming her pleasure, she reached up and pinched her nipples until they both came. She sat astride him, panting. His dick barely softened when she sat up again and, for the second time, fucked him until they both came.

"Wow," she said. "You're fabulous."

Me? he thought. *I didn't do a thing.* She climbed off him.

Come dripping over his balls, he slowly sat up. "You're pretty good yourself."

"I couldn't resist you. You're just soooo sexy."

Irresistible. Holy shit!

"I have to get home," Sharon said. "Will I see you tomorrow?"

Hmm. Fuck and run? Talk about slam, bam. Oh well, he was more than satisfied. "I don't know," he said. How would she react to him without the potion? He vowed to himself that she'd never have the chance to find out. He would be at the little shop when it opened and get a supply of the irresistibility potion, no matter the cost.

Potions:
The Reorder

❧

*T*HE FOLLOWING MORNING, DALE WAS AT THE GRIMY LIT-
tle shop before nine. He had no idea what its hours were, but
he'd called in to work saying he'd be late and he was determined to stand in front until the shop opened.

He didn't know what more of the irresistibility potion
would cost, but whatever it was, he'd manage. After the way
Sharon had reacted the previous evening, he was hooked.
Precisely at nine the little man arrived and opened the front
door. "I was pretty sure you'd be here bright and early."
He grinned, showing his slightly yellowed teeth. "Worked,
didn't it?"

"That's an understatement." He shouldn't make it so

obvious that he was going to buy more since it would inevitably drive up the price. However, he'd been unable to keep the shit-eating grin off his face since he got out of Sharon's car.

"I told you so."

"That you did."

"Well, come in, come in, and I'll get you some more." Little bell tinkling, he walked back into the shop, with Dale right behind.

Almost afraid to ask, but willing to pay any price, he said, "How much will more cost me?"

"Not much," Mr. Dearly said. "Not much at all." When Dale remained silent, Mr. Dearly said, "I'll only dispense a week's worth at a time." He shuffled over and pulled the bottle from the shelf. Taking a larger tube from another shelf he walked over to the counter and filled it carefully with the liquid, topping the vial with a cork. Handing it to Dale, he said, "That will be twenty dollars."

Shocked, Dale said, "Only twenty dollars?" Dumb thing to say, he realized when the words were out of his mouth, but the guy could have charged him a hundred, or even a thousand.

"That's it. I would suggest that you use it sparingly. There's an interesting facet to this particular potion. Many men find that the effects last longer and longer each time. You'll have to see how it works for you."

Still almost speechless, he reached into his wallet and handed Mr. Dearly two ten-dollar bills and walked out of the store, vial again lodged safely in his shirt pocket. *Maybe he does make his money on reorders,* Dale thought. After all, he'd certainly be back every week for more, and at twenty dollars a pop, he could easily afford it. How many other men arrived at the shop each week for reorders? After all, how much did it actually cost to keep up that tired little shop?

At home, he got ready for work, dabbing a little of the liquid behind each ear. Looking at his watch he realized that he'd only be an hour late. His boss might object but the hell with her. She'd been on his case for weeks and it didn't seem to matter what he did. But he needed the job.

He took the bus to his office and got into the elevator. Three women were chatting as they got on after him. He pressed the button for the third floor and looked at the women, asking with his glance which floor they wanted. The elevator doors slid shut and the car began to rise.

"That's okay, I'll get it," one said, pressing herself against him as she reached for the button.

"I'll get it," another said, pushing her friend out of the way and rubbing against him like a cat in heat.

"Get out of my way," the third said, grabbing him around the waist and rubbing her pubic bone against his hip.

"Ladies," he said as the door opened at his floor. "I have to get off here."

As he walked down the hallway, he heard the women squabbling. *Damn, this potion does it to everyone. I'm an incredibly lucky man.*

He entered his office and was greeted by several of the guys. "How did last evening go?" Steve asked.

All he did was grin.

"Mr. Conroy," his boss yelled through the open door to her office. "Nice of you to show up."

He crossed the room and entered her tiny office. "I'm so sorry, Ms. Tompkins, I had an errand to run."

Without a word, she rose, crossed to the door, and closed it firmly. "That's fine, Dale." She flipped the lock. "No harm done."

She slowly ran the palms of her hands down the hips of her tight black skirt, then began to unbutton her bright blue blouse. Button by button the sides of the blouse parted, revealing a satiny, light blue bra, and the swollen nipples of her small, compact breasts beneath. She said nothing as she moved so her body pressed against his. He backed up slightly and found himself almost sitting on the edge of her desk, staring at her tits.

She reached behind her and unfastened the clasp and removed both her blouse and bra. She offered him one tit. "Suck," she said simply.

He obliged, hands massaging her flesh. As her head fell back, he filled his mouth with her, inhaling the subtle fragrance of her arousal.

As he sucked, she unfastened her skirt and let it fall to the floor, followed by her panties.

"Leave the rest on," Dale said, holding her from him and gazing at her dark stockings and high-heeled black shoes.

"Of course," she whispered, voice husky with arousal. She quickly opened his belt and unbuttoned and unzipped until his slacks were around his ankles. She pushed him backward until he was lying across her desk and she was mounting him, one foot on the floor and the other knee beside his hip.

She pounded onto him, driving his cock into her body over and over, hands everywhere, rubbing his chest through his shirt, cupping his sac, scratching his inner thighs with her long, perfectly polished nails. They turned over and Dale fucked her with enthusiasm.

They each came twice.

Finally they straightened and she got tissues from her desk drawer. "We have to get cleaned up," she said. "Then I guess we should get to work. Later?"

Totally flummoxed, he nodded, wiped semen and her juices from his body, and re-dressed.

"Did you get fired?" Steve asked when he emerged.

"Nope," he said, keeping his own counsel.

He was almost attacked by a woman in the elevator on his way to lunch and several women followed him into the park and tried to sit beside him on a bench. He had to keep moving and ate his hot dog while walking. For a change, he wasn't interested in any more quickies. He kept to himself until mid-afternoon when he was called into Ms. Tompkins's office for another round of hot, steamy fucking.

As he left the office at five o'clock, he found himself looking around, making sure there were no women in the vicinity. *I'll have to use much less tomorrow*, he thought. *This is a little ridiculous.*

The following morning, he thought about doing without, but he couldn't resist dabbing only a tiny amount behind one ear. After all, he had enjoyed the quickies in Ms. Tompkins's office. God, she was gorgeous and watching her get down and dirty was truly hot.

He entered her office and she again closed and locked the door. This time he wanted to see if he could get her to suck him off until he came. As she turned from the door, he unzipped his pants. He'd deliberately gone commando so there were no shorts to get in his way. He leaned against the desk and said, "Suck me off."

Her breath caught in her throat and she said, "Of course." On her knees she took him deep into her mouth and created a vacuum. Then she pulled back and sucked him in deep again. Cupping his testicles and scratching the tender area between his balls and anus, she kept sucking until he spurted into her throat.

"Do me, please," she begged, pulling up her skirt and sitting on the edge of her desk. Like Sharon had, she'd left off her panties. Her pussy was swollen and glistening with her juices. "Please?" she said.

He was only too happy to oblige. He pulled up a chair and settled in, licking her engorged clit and fingering her hole. It took only a minute for her to come, clamping her thighs against his ears. He kept licking and she kept coming. Finally, exhausted, she pushed him away and slid off the desk, saying, "Later."

Dale stayed in and ate peanut butter crackers from the vending machine for lunch. Dodging women was becoming a pain.

Over the next few days, he dabbed on less and less of the potion until he stopped using it altogether. It didn't seem to matter. Women kept attacking him. Several catfights had broken out among women wanting to rub up against him. Every morning and afternoon he fucked or was fucked by his boss. He was unable to meet his friends for dinner because Sharon made more and more demands on him.

Amazingly enough, his cock was sore and he was getting tired of fucking. He couldn't even talk with a woman without dire consequences. And now the effect seemed to be permanent.

About two weeks after his first visit, Dale returned to the little shop. Mr. Dearly was behind the counter serving another customer. "It really works like that?" the man asked.

"It certainly does. Just ask this customer," he said, pointing to Dale. "The irresistibility potion works the way I said, doesn't it?"

"It does, but—"

Mr. Dearly cut him off. "You see? And the first day's potion is free."

"What would it cost from then on?" the man asked.

"Only twenty dollars a week. And sometimes you don't even need more. The effect seems to be cumulative. Right?" he said to Dale.

"In truth. I don't need to use any now," Dale said, "but there is something—"

Again Mr. Dearly interrupted him. "So take this and see what happens," he said to his customer, who smiled and pocketed his little tube.

The little bell tinkled as he left the store. Mr. Dearly turned to Dale. "Now, what can I do for you?"

"I've got a little problem."

Mr. Dearly's eyes widened. "Don't tell me it's stopped working."

"Exactly the opposite. It seems permanent. I can't turn it off."

"Is that bad?"

"It's getting to be a pain. I can't have any kind of relationship with women. All they want is sex. There's no way I can talk with them, go to a movie, bowl. It's getting annoying."

"I'm so sorry."

"Can you turn it off?"

"I have a reversal formula. A sort of resistibility potion."

Dale let out a long, relieved sigh. "That's great. I need some."

Mr. Dearly shuffled to another shelf and took down a small bottle. "Just a few drops of this behind each ear will cancel the effects of the irresistibility potion." He poured a small amount into a vial but he didn't hand it to Dale. "That will be five hundred dollars."

"What?" The word exploded from Dale's mouth.

"You'll pay it, won't you?" He leered. "Of course you will."

"But everything else was so cheap."

The smile on Mr. Dearly's face was almost evil. "It's always the same. Men have no idea what irresistibility will do. And when they want it reversed, well, that's how I keep my little shop going. That's why my name is Pay Dearly." His laugh was almost maniacal, but Dale paid.

The new potion worked as Pay Dearly had promised. Now Dale had a lot to think about.

Friday Night Games: The Awakening

❧

SCOTT AND I LOVE TO PLAY GAMES. SEXY GAMES. WE'VE been married for almost three years, no kids, and at first we had a plain vanilla sex life. The change started about a year ago when Scott was surfing the 'Net and came across a website devoted to off-center sex activities. Although back then we were both pretty naive about the games people play, we were very open about discussing sex.

"Uh, Lynn, come in here and take a look at this," he called that first Friday evening, a slight hesitation in his voice. Curious, I wandered into the den where our computer was set up. And I looked. Some of the pictures he flipped through took my breath away—and tightened my nipples and made my pussy twitch.

"Real people don't do stuff like that," I said. The *stuff* on the screen at that moment was a picture of an ordinary-looking woman, leaning over the back of a sofa, naked ass already reddened by the hand of the man poised over her. "Do they?"

Scott raised his eyebrows. "This site claims to feature amateurs."

"Riiight," I said, not believing a word of it, but also slightly breathless. "Amateurs who get paid to do this stuff."

"Who cares whether they're really professionals or not?" he said, still staring at the screen. "It's still really hot." He paged forward to another photo, showing a different couple, a man, fully clothed, sitting on a straight chair with a woman draped over his knees. While she was dressed from the waist up, her butt was naked, positioned for spanking. His hand was raised and, if you looked closely (and I did), her rear was red as was his palm. *Boy, have I been living in a sheltered environment,* I thought. Whether these people were "just folks" or paid, obviously viewers enjoyed seeing photos like this. I was speechless, shocked both at the photos and my innocence.

Scott moved his mouse and clicked to another photo, one that showed a naked woman positioned over a bench, wrists and ankles tied to its legs, a man standing menacingly over her, a Ping-Pong paddle in his hand. This man was naked and his arousal was all too obvious. It was probably posed, but I had to admit that it was exciting me.

"You really think it's hot?" I said, a little tentatively. *Does he want me to participate in something like these photos show?*

"Sure." He reached up and tweaked one of my erect nipples. "And obviously you do, too." He all but dragged me to the bedroom, stripped me bare, and, with no preamble, fucked me hard and fast. As I was about to come, Scott slapped my ass. Once. It wasn't a hard slap, but I both heard and felt it, and I came really quickly—amazingly quickly. God, I'd been so aroused. And the little bit of pain, and the surprise of it, threw me over the edge.

It was quite a while before I could speak a coherent sentence. "That was—quite something," I said, trying to catch my breath and not exactly sure what to say.

"Oh, yeah," he said, panting. "Quite something, indeed." He lifted himself on one elbow and looked down at me. "And there's so much more, if you want to try some stuff."

Enlightenment dawned. "I would guess," I said, now calmer, "that this isn't the first time you visited that site."

His long sigh was my answer. "No, it isn't. I was intrigued by something one of the guys at work said a while ago, and so I searched the web. I've been looking at sites like that one for a few weeks, and I've been really excited by some of the photos I've seen." He gazed at me seriously. "I just didn't know how to broach the subject with you."

I swallowed, still unsure how I should react. "I can imagine."

"You seemed to enjoy, uhh, things."

I took a deep breath and let it out slowly. *Okay,* I told myself, *knee-jerk would be to deny. Be a good girl. None of that kinky stuff for Mommy's little girl.* And yet . . . "I guess I did," I said tentatively.

Scott's slow release of breath was the sound of his relief. "I've wanted to play the occasional game with you but—even talking about this is a little scary. I was afraid you'd think I was some kind of a freak."

I cupped his cheek with my hand and took the plunge. I've been grateful ever since that I did. "It is scary, but isn't that some of the fun of it?"

His grin said it all. "Yeah, I guess it is."

"I don't know whether I'm into anything as heavy as what was in those pictures, but maybe we've let things get a little"—I searched for a word that wouldn't hurt his feelings, or mine—"predictable."

"Maybe it's time we added a few different things," he said. "Games, maybe. You know . . ."

I saw a whole bunch of new opportunities. "I don't know yet, but let's see what we can think of."

We talked a few times that weekend and decided to begin slowly. The swat on my ass had been erotic, but I didn't know whether I could deal with it when I had time to consider. We worried briefly about the slight stress of trying to fulfill each other's desires and vowed not to do anything "for the other guy," but only play games we thought we'd enjoy ourselves. And we promised that we'd call anything off at any time.

We decided to play on Friday nights, trying to start the weekend off with a bang. Literally. At first we kept it simple.

"How about playing hooker and customer?" I suggested a few days later. "That way, if you pay me, you can ask for anything."

Scott's expression of pleasure and his slow nodding as he digested what I said was my answer. Then he got serious. "And you can refuse, right?"

I nodded. "Right."

"Please, Lynn, you have to be able to say no. Otherwise I can't ask for anything we haven't discussed in advance."

He was right. I was going to be an unusual hooker who would easily refuse a "customer's" wishes. "You're right. I promise that I will say no if I don't want to play."

I bought what I thought would be a sexy, hooker-type outfit from a website, and the following Friday evening, I dressed in the bedroom while he waited in the living room. We'd agreed only on the basics. He had some funny money with which to pay me but that was about all we knew. So, as I walked into the living room we had only the beginning of the scene choreographed. "Madam Carrie said you wanted some company."

Scott's eyes nearly bugged out of his head when he saw me. I was wearing a tiny pair of lacy black panties with little red knots around the top and a black bra with matching red ribbons, tied in a bow at the front of each cup. I had combined the pair with a black garter belt and long, black fishnet stockings, and black shoes with four-inch heels. I had put on more makeup that I usually wear, with heavy mascara, shadow, and eyeliner, as well as bright red lipstick. "My name's Tina, but you can call me whatever you like." I struck what I hoped would be a hooker-like pose with one foot on the coffee table, one hand on my hip, pelvis and breasts thrust forward. I was a little embarrassed at first but the wonderful look on Scott's face made me feel stronger.

I watched my husband blink convulsively then swallow hard. "Hello, Tina."

"Hi, Scott." I gathered my courage and walked close to him. "Will I do for company tonight?"

"God, yes," he said, already gasping for air. "Definitely."

I reached down and pressed the heel of my hand against the front of his jeans. "I guess so." I straddled his thighs and sat on his lap, facing him, rubbing my pubic bone against his thighs. *Not too fast,* I told myself. I was in no hurry and I hoped he wasn't either.

I leaned over and brushed my fingertip over his lips, my breasts spilling over the top of the one-cup-size-too-small bra. I watched his eyes flick to my tits, then back to my face. The bra had a push-'em-up-and-together feature so it created lots more cleavage than I really have. I cupped my breasts and rubbed them lightly against his shirt front.

While I slid my lips over his, I unbuttoned his shirt and exposed his bare chest, then I brushed my lace-and-satin-covered tits against his bare skin. He reached one hand behind me to pull my body more tightly against him and the other cupped the back of my head while he kissed me deeply.

Long moments of sexual playing had us both eager so I leaned back. "Did you pay Madam Carrie for any—extra services? She didn't tell me the details."

"Extra services?"

"Everything here costs extra. The basic rate is just for a little of this, then into the bedroom and, well, doing it."

Scott pulled a wad of bills from his pocket. "This ought to cover whatever we decide to do."

We. I liked that. "This should get you whatever you want." I took all the money and tucked it into the top of one stocking.

"Let's see what these bows do," he said, fondling my breasts. He untied the red knots and discovered that small openings at the front of each cup exposed my already firm nipples. He leaned over and flicked the tips lightly, then he bit me.

I jumped. It hurt, but felt really exciting, too. Juice flowed freely from my now sopping crotch. God, it was electric. When he bit the other, I let my head fall back and thrust out my chest. Now he was tugging at one and pinching the other. I thought I'd come right then.

"Now," he said, moving me slightly so he could unzip the fly of his jeans. His steel-hard cock stuck out from the opening. "I don't want to wait." Quickly he pulled the minuscule crotch of my panties aside, lifted me by the hips, and dropped me on his dick. I was so wet that I could hear a squishy sound as he fucked me.

I squeezed my vaginal muscles to try to give him more pleasure, but he was too far gone to care. "Shit, shit, shit," he cried as his hips bucked and he came inside me.

Almost immediately he flipped me over onto my back on the sofa, pulled off the panties, and fastened his mouth on my dripping pussy. As he sucked my clit, his fingers found my hole. He sucked and rammed his fingers in and out until I came, screaming.

It was a long time before I could catch my breath. "Holy cow," I said.

"Oh yeah," Scott sighed. "Holy cow, indeed."

Since then . . . Well, I'll write more later. For now, just telling the story of that first Friday night has made me so hot that I think I'll go inside and jump Scott's bones, even though it's only Tuesday.

Friday Night Games:
Learning More

❦

As I told you last time, Scott and I had gotten into game playing. We began with hooker and customer and played that scenario in one form or another for about a month. The first time we were so excited that we fucked almost immediately, but gradually we were able to stretch out the foreplay so we could get adventurous. Oral sex had always formed a wonderful part of our lovemaking and, since I was being "paid" for my services, he asked me to play with his balls or stroke the area between his balls and anus. I learned a lot from the requests he made of his hooker.

Anyway, one Friday evening he made an unusual request. I had increased my wardrobe, and that evening I was wearing a red bustier that laced up the front and left my pussy bare, with red thigh-high hose and red hooker heels, all of which I'd ordered from my favorite adults-only website. "Tina," he said, calling me by my hooker name, "I'd like to do something a little different tonight."

Fine with me. I'd looked around on the web and dispelled much of my earlier naïveté. There was so much out there to play with and I was always interested in expanding our horizons, finding out what we would enjoy. "If you've got the money, I'm game."

He said, softly, "I'd like to spank your bottom."

Our adventures had begun with photos of spanking and he occasionally swatted my bottom when we climaxed, but it had gone no further than that. Was I up for this? "As long as either of us can call it off," I said, not as Tina but as myself.

"I insist on that," he said.

"Good," I said, extending my hand, palm up. "Let's see the cash."

He reached into his pocket and handed me a wad of phony money. As always I tucked it into the top of one stocking. "Is that enough?"

"For anything you want," I responded.

"Good. Come over here," he said, settling on a living room chair. As I stood beside him he groped my pussy. "You know, it's really evil for you to go around tempting nice men like me." He tugged on my pubic hair. "Leaving your snatch bare is an invitation."

I giggled but remained silent.

He grabbed my wrist. "I'm going to punish you for everything you've been doing." He pulled me and, off balance, I fell over his lap, ass in the air. He reached into the top of my teddy and scooped out my breasts so they hung against his calf. Holding me down with his other arm, he tugged rhythmically at my nipples. Then he ran his fingers through my snatch. "I knew you were a very bad girl. This all makes you very wet."

He was right about everything. I was trembling with excitement. "You need to cool off a bit." He brought the palm of his hand down onto one cheek with a smack.

I jumped. It hurt only a little, but the pain seemed to extend tendrils of heat to my clit. He rubbed my ass then smacked me again. It quickly became an odd combination of pain and extreme pleasure, which wound around each other as he alternately slapped me and played with my breasts and pussy.

As happened the first time we played hooker and customer, our patience was limited. After only a few smacks, he tossed me onto the floor, pulled off his jeans, and pounded into me. The feel of the carpet on my sore bottom only added to my arousal.

With only a few thrusts we came almost simultaneously.

Friday Night Games:
Growing

❧

𝒯HE FRIDAY AFTER MY HUSBAND, SCOTT, AND I, IN MY PER-
sona as Tina the hooker, made love on the living room floor
after he spanked me the first time, our playing began in a
similar way. I arrived in the living room, and Scott paid me
my fee. I wore the same red teddy with the bare crotch and
he again told me what a bad girl I was for tempting nice men
like him. It was all I could do not to laugh. Nice, indeed.
He had a most deliciously evil mind and I appreciated every
deviant thought.

I played along, waiting for him to sit then position me over
his lap. Instead he guided me to the coffee table. "Tonight
I've prepared for you, Tina," he said. "You don't seem to
have learned from last week's lesson, so I've decided you need

to be taught in a different way." He moved me until I stood at one narrow end of the wooden table.

Scott had obviously been thinking about this for a while and there was a grin in his voice.

"I want to get serious for a moment," he said to his wife. "This isn't for Tina, but for Lynn."

"Okay," I said, now wary.

"I want to play games tonight. I've been touring a lot of websites and lots of activities I saw there turned me on. I think many will turn you on, too. However." He cupped my chin and raised my gaze until I looked directly into his eyes. "However, we both need to promise to call it off at any time if we're uncomfortable."

"I thought we'd already agreed to that."

"We did, but I want to reinforce it. I want to be free to try things. Some you might not enjoy. Please, tell me."

"Sure," I said readily agreeing.

"If you promise to say something, I promise to stop. Deal?"

He was taking this all so seriously, and that was one of the many reasons I loved him. "Deal," I said.

"In much of my reading, couples had words they could use to stop anything and everything." When I looked puzzled, he continued, "If you want to say 'Oh, please don't,' for effect, then you can say it. If you really want to stop, though, how about—" He looked around the room. "How about *coffeepot*? If you say that, I'll stop. Agreed?"

I took a deep breath. "Sounds like you've got some pretty kinky stuff in mind."

He waggled his eyebrows. "Maybe I do. Coffeepot. Yes?"

"Coffeepot it is." We shook on it.

"Okay. Now lie down. I want you for my plaything."

I remembered a photo we'd seen on a website and realized that Scott recalled it, too. I squeaked as I settled on my back on the cold wood. "It's freezing."

"We'll warm it up soon enough." He took a small box from behind the sofa and put it on the floor beside him. "I've been doing a little shopping."

"I see." But I didn't; I couldn't see inside the box.

"I went to an adult website and bought a few things. Hold out your arms, and remember our word."

I nodded and held out my arms. From the box, Scott took two plastic- and cardboard-wrapped packages and, using a pair of scissors, removed the packaging. He brandished two pairs of black, fur-lined handcuffs. "Okay?"

I was game so again I nodded. It was sweet that he needed constant reassurance. I guess I would, too, if the roles were reversed. He quickly fastened one cuff to each wrist, leaving the other end dangling. From the box he removed two more larger ones, and efficiently clasped them onto my ankles.

"One more thing," he said, pulling out a pair of black wooden clothespin-looking things I assumed were nipple clamps, connected with a metal chain. I'd seen them in many of the pictures Scott had shown me on the web. "Ready?"

I sighed, willing to try. "As ready as I'll ever be." I knew how erotic I found the spankings I'd been given and I hoped the clamps would increase the sensations.

He clipped them on. "If they are too tight there's an adjustment."

I felt the sensation throughout my body. Pain, yes. But excitement, too. They might get too tight over time but for the moment I was all right with it.

"Okay, lie on the table, facedown."

When I was as comfortable as I was going to get, with the nipple clamps beneath me, I told Scott I was ready, and he fastened the free end of each of the four sets of handcuffs to the legs of the table. "I was afraid the hardware underneath you would be uncomfortable in a bad way so I brought a pillow." He lifted my chest and butt and slid a thick foam cushion beneath my pubis. It had the effect of letting my breasts hang slightly and lessened the discomfort of the equipment beneath me. "And, of course, it puts your ass right where I want it."

I was becoming lost in the sea of sensations and couldn't say anything.

My face was turned toward the center of the room where I could watch Scott unwrap yet another toy, a black wooden paddle. "Ready for this?"

I could only nod.

"Maybe only five, but you can say *coffeepot* at any time." He sat on the sofa beside me, and I turned to watch him. He raised the paddle and swatted my ass. It wasn't a love tap, but I knew he could paddle me harder if he wanted. "That's one."

He stopped and stroked my ass. Then he swatted me again. "That's two."

By then my pussy was twitching, and as my nipples swelled, the clamps got tighter.

Again the paddle fell. "That's three."

I was trembling with arousal. I watched Scott move to the foot of the table and felt his fingers in my pussy. "So wet," he crooned. "I've got something for that."

Again he went to the box, this time withdrawing a large dildo with a wire attached. He rubbed the cold plastic over my folds, then pushed it inside me. "With your ass in the air this should stay in place," he said.

If he'd played with that phallus a bit I'd have come right then, but I couldn't get enough stimulation from the unmoving thing to push me over the edge. I clenched and released my vaginal muscles but I couldn't quite do it.

Again the paddle landed, only increasing my excitement. The nipple clamps hurt more now, and the pleasure I'd had from them earlier changed to just plain pain. I considered not calling it quits, but decided that if Scott couldn't trust me, he wouldn't feel as free to experiment. "Coffeepot."

"Baby," Scott said, sounding totally contrite. "I'm so sorry." He started to unfasten my wrists but I stopped him. Minutes ago I couldn't have uttered a full sentence but the pain was bringing me back to life. "No, Scott. Not that. Just unclip these nipple things and don't stop."

He quickly removed the clamps, then, without pause, hit my ass hard. I jumped and almost came. "About this thing in your pussy. It does tricks."

I heard and felt a buzzing in my cunt, then the dildo actually moved. I came then, screaming, moaning. "Yes! Yes! Yes!"

My body collapsed and Scott withdrew the toy. My ass stung, but he spread a cooling lotion on my flesh. He then removed the cuffs and pulled me to the carpet between his thighs. I had to move only slightly to unzip his jeans and pull out his rock-hard cock. I licked and sucked until, with a matching scream, he came.

We both stretched out on the sofa. Later I again reassured Scott that I had enjoyed our playing. "As if my very noisy climax wasn't enough for you."

He laughed. "And you realized how excited it made me as well."

"You don't often come in my mouth," I said, giggling.

"Too true." He laughed with me. "You didn't mind, did you?"

"Not in the least."

"Does that mean we can do this again sometime?"

My smile lit my face. "You're damned right we can. One last thing. Anytime you want to shop on the 'Net, you've got my wholehearted approval. Some things won't work out but lots will."

"I want to try so many things."

"Go for it, with my enthusiastic support. Maybe I'll do some toy shopping, too."

Vivid Dreaming

⟡

I GUESS IT'S ONE OF THE MEDICATIONS I'M TAKING. IT doesn't matter why I'm taking stuff; suffice it to say, I'm feeling great now. Anyway, something has caused me to have vivid dreams. Not nightmares, just really detailed, realistic dreams. I mean dreams that feel so real that it's difficult to accept that I'm awake afterward. Most are truly benign. I'm taking the kids to school, or I'm having dinner at Mac's parent's house. Like that. Not sexy, just . . . there. However . . .

I was in bed and really horny. It was deep winter and I was a little chilly, so I snuggled against Mac and enjoyed the feel of his warm, firm, sexy body against mine. Sexy body? It's the middle of the night and he's snoring away yet I'm thinking *sexy*. What the heck should I do?

First, I told myself I was dreaming, and I sort of knew I was. I opened my eyes and I was in the room I grew up in as a kid at my folks' house. But I was in a double bed, while my bed as a child was a single. And I felt like a teenager, not like a thirty-five-year-old stay-at-home mom.

I looked over and Mac was in the bed with me, although he looked like the Mac I had met almost eighteen years before. I smiled. What we wouldn't have given back then for a bed and time to enjoy it. I felt as horny and frustrated as I had back then, although I knew I was dreaming. Confusing.

Okay, so in my dream Mac woke up and rolled me over. I could hear his heavy breathing and I wondered whether it was from just being awakened or from arousal. I wanted it to be arousal. You can bet on that.

He grabbed me by the front of my nightgown and pulled my face to his. Again, I knew it was a dream. In the real world, I don't wear nightgowns. Maybe I should've wanted to wake up, but his lips felt so good. I love it when he's forceful and he made it plain that he wanted what he wanted, and what he wanted was me. Right then!

He tangled his fingers in my long hair (another indication that this wasn't real) and held my lips against his. He was rough, holding me tightly and not letting me move away, and I felt my nipples tighten until they were almost painful. And he didn't stop kissing me until I wanted to seize his hand and put in on my aching tits.

Eventually, he released me and bit my left nipple lightly.

I wasn't even surprised that my nightgown had suddenly disappeared. He sucked and bit until I was driven almost to distraction. He moved from breast to breast, being aggressive and masterful, just the way I liked it. My nipples were wet from his mouth's ministrations. When I reached out to hold his face against me he grabbed my hands and held them over my head, still using his mouth on my tits.

My pussy was sopping by then, and I couldn't keep my thighs still. I rubbed my legs together to try to ease the pressure. Then his hand was there, stroking the insides of my thighs. Although I didn't think I could get more excited, the contrast between the gentle stroking and the hard sucking drove me higher still.

"Touch me, please," I begged. I needed what I knew his fingers could do, and he knew it. I could hear his light chuckle. God, if only this weren't a dream. Mac hadn't been like this in years. Oh well . . . I vowed to enjoy the dream and masturbate afterward, if necessary.

His fingers found my clit and it took only a few caresses for me to come. The strength of the spasms surprised me. Hard. Long. So hot. My arousal diminished only slightly as his fingers continued to play with my clit. Had I come? I knew I had but my body was just as hot as it had been.

One finger entered my sopping pussy while his thumb rubbed my clit. I came again. I was sorry for that, since, on the few occasions that I've climaxed twice, I came down really fast.

Not so tonight, in this marvelous, realistic dream. I was still soooo hungry.

I started to reach for Mac, but he pushed my hand away. He wanted to do it all, and who was I to argue? His fingers played with my clit and my cunt lips while his teeth nibbled on my tits and his tongue wet my flesh.

With a low growl, Mac pushed me onto my stomach, grabbed my hips to raise my rear, then entered me from behind, doggie-style. He wasted no time on any more pre-liminaries, but pulled out, then plunged into me again, big and hard and so wonderful. I needed him so much and his cock filled me. He reached beneath me, pulled at my nipples and fingered my clit. I came yet a third time. I've never done that before.

"This is amazing. I can actually feel your climax," he said, his voice hoarse. He continued to pound into me until he came, his dick deep inside me, pouring his jism into my body.

Panting, he rolled off of me and pulled me close against his side. *Please*, I thought, *I don't want to wake up yet.*

"God, that was amazing," I purred.

"It was that," Mac rumbled.

I opened my eyes and looked at him. I was startled to see that it was my Mac, thirty-seven, hairline beginning to recede, a totally bemused look on his face. I glanced around. It was my bedroom in the house Mac and I had bought eight years ago.

Am I awake now? I was totally confused. There was no

denying that orgasm. I was leaking between my legs, making a wet spot on the bed.

"I loved that," Mac said, his speech becoming slurred with impending sleep. "When you grabbed me from a sound sleep, it took only moments for me to get hard. Do that more often, will you?" He yawned and in moments I could hear his regular breathing become deeper and more even.

What had happened? Where had the dream ended and reality begun? I tried to figure it out, then decided that it didn't matter. Mac and I had just had some of the hottest sex we'd had since we were first married. Why overthink this? I just knew that the next time I woke up in the middle of the night I would grab him again and try to replay tonight. Wow!! How fabulous!

Shaving

*T*T ALL BEGAN IN MY SENIOR YEAR IN COLLEGE. My LIVING
arrangements sucked, so I answered an ad from a woman
looking for a roommate. I was delighted with both the small
house and the twentysomething brunette who would live
there with me. The cost was doable and I quickly gave Carrie
a check for the first and last month's rent.

"I'm delighted you're going to be moving in, Angie," she
said. "When Pauline broke her leg and moved back home I
thought I'd have to carry the whole rent myself." She hugged
me quickly, grabbed her cell phone, and told several friends
about our new arrangement.

I moved in a day later and settled in easily. We quickly

became fast friends and, although I had my own bathroom, Carrie and I comfortably shared the kitchen and living room. Neither of us were party people so, when not with our respective boyfriends, we spent many an evening in front of the TV together watching reality shows or rented movies.

Things changed just before Thanksgiving. Her shower was larger than the one in my bathroom and one afternoon I'd been caught in the rain and took advantage of her absence to use it, accidentally leaving my shampoo and body wash behind.

Needing my stuff back, the following afternoon I knocked on her bathroom door and, hearing nothing, walked in. I entered and there was Carrie, her well-shaped body wet and naked, stepping from the shower. "It's fine," she said. "No sweat," she said as she saw my hesitation. "You came for your stuff. I meant to put everything back in your bathroom but I forgot." She motioned. "It's all on the back of the john."

I stuttered a bit when I realized that, although we'd lived together for almost three months, we'd not seen each other naked before. I wasn't embarrassed, it was merely awkward.

My gaze dropped to her crotch area, and I was startled to realize that she'd shaved her pubic hair. When she followed my stare she laughed. "Tommy loves me this way, so I shave almost every day."

"God," I said as Carrie casually wrapped herself in a towel. "Jeff would go bonkers. Once in a while we rent a porno flick and he ogles the naked pussies."

"So why don't you shave?"

Why? "I thought it would be icky. Doesn't it get all itchy and stubbly?"

"Not if you're careful. I use before- and aftershave stuff and haven't had any problems."

My body reacted to the thought of my boyfriend's reaction. "Jeff would jump me in a New York minute if I did that."

"So? Go for it. You're welcome to borrow what you need."

"Can I do it myself?"

"I've been shaving for almost a year and it's become second nature for me. For you, it would be good if someone showed you the ropes. You could always let Jeff do it."

I though of Jeff's huge football-player hands. "I'd be afraid to let him touch me like that. Sex is one thing, but shaving my pussy? He'd be all thumbs."

Carrie raised a questioning eyebrow. "I could do it for you the first time if you'd like."

"You would?"

And that was how it started. "Sure. I don't have the time right now," she said, rubbing her hair dry. "You available late afternoon tomorrow?"

"Jeff is picking me up around six. Would we be done by then?"

"I can leave my office at four so we could start around four thirty. Your last class is at two, right? So that should work."

"Great. Anything I should get?"

"I've got everything. If you get here before I do, take a long hot shower and we'll make Jeff drool."

The following afternoon, by the time I was done in the shower Carrie was in her bedroom arranging several items on her night stand. "My tools," she said.

Wrapped in a towel, I looked at all the stuff she'd gathered. She had creams, lotions, a pair of scissors, and a razor. "Okay. What should I do?"

"Unless it makes you uncomfortable, lose the towel and lie across the bed with your legs off the edge over here." As I settled she said, "You've got a great body, by the way. I've always liked the way you wear your clothes, but I've never seen you completely nude before. Not bad at all."

"Thanks," I said, a little embarrassed by her praise.

"No sweat," she said lightly. Then she picked up the scissors. "First I need to trim your bush really short. The only thing you need to do is hold still. Very still."

"Believe me, I won't move a muscle."

While she trimmed my pubic hair the only sound in the room was the snick of the scissors. At one point the cold metal touched the inside of my thigh and I gasped, but kept entirely unmoving.

When she was done, she said, "Okay. I have some softening lotion that will make the razor work much better." She began to apply something mildly aromatic all over my groin. I was a little abashed to realize that her ministrations were arousing me.

I'd never been with a woman and I didn't think I had any lesbian in me, but erotic touches were erotic touches and my pussy began to tingle. Seeming oblivious to my excitement, Carrie then smoothed shaving cream on my parts.

"This is a new razor and I advise you to use a fresh disposable every time. Again, don't move!"

I held still and the feel of the long, slow strokes of the blade only added to my arousal. Then I felt her fingers delving into my folds. Suddenly I didn't think that shaving my pussy was all she was doing. She'd told me not to move so I used that as a mental excuse not to stop her.

"You're being very good," Carrie said, her breath hot on my newly bare skin. "Not moving and all. I'm not hurting you, am I?"

My nipples contracted and I began to pant. "No," I managed to say.

"Good," she said, her voice soft and breathy. Her fingers slipped through my totally wet flesh, now lubricated with my juices. "Have you ever done anything like this before?"

I knew she meant played sexually with a woman. Not mis-understanding, I answered, "No."

Her fingers playing with my inner lips, Carrie said, "I want you to know that I'm not a homosexual. Rather, I love sex, with guys and occasionally with women as well."

"I've never . . ."

"I realize that." She paused. "If you want me to stop, I will."

I thought a minute. "No," I said softly. "As long as it won't ruin our friendship."

"Why would it?" she said. "Just relax."

Her thumbs parted me and her mouth found my slit, her teeth nipping at my swollen flesh, one forefinger slowly invading me. I wanted to say something but I was totally incapable of speech. Her hot breath flowed over my bare, wet skin as a second finger joined the first, filling me, as her lips found my clit. She sucked and in only a few moments I could hold back no longer. Waves of orgasm flowed over me caus-ing all my muscles to clench and my toes to curl. I couldn't catch my breath and I felt my pulse pound in my ears.

She kept licking and sucking until I began to calm. When I could speak, I said, "Shit. That was a surprise."

"A good one I hope," Carrie said.

"A very good one."

"I'm glad. However, this means you need to take another shower to wash off all the, well, let's just say leftovers, and then I'll finish with some aftershave lotion."

Still breathing rapidly but trying to sound calm I asked, "When will I have to do this again?"

"I shave every day or so, and I'll be glad to help you next time."

I raised my head and looked into Carrie's eyes. "I hope you will."

The Painting

ELLIE HAD BOUGHT THE PAINTING AT A NEIGHBORHOOD tag sale. She wasn't sure exactly what had appealed to her about the swirls of reds and blacks, but something in the abstract design spoke to her and, after she bargained the owner down to twenty dollars, she'd bought it.

Now, in her tiny apartment, she was thinking about where to hang it. She had no wall space in her minuscule living room, so she carried it into the bedroom. No place there, either. She realized that her impulse purchase had probably been a waste of money, but she somehow couldn't bear to part with it. She cleared a little space on her dresser and propped it against the mirror. "For the moment," she said aloud, "you'll live here. I can use the bathroom mirror when I need to."

That evening she lay on her bed, feet pointing toward the painting, just gazing into the central swirl. For a moment it seemed to be moving, like some kind of special-effects vortex. *Don't be silly*, she told herself, *you've got a little Spielberg in your brain.*

But it did seem to be spinning slowly. As she watched, the painting dissolved into the form of a man. He wasn't looking at her, rather standing in profile in what looked like a bedroom. *Okay*, she told herself, *no more pepperoni pizzas for you!*

He was there, however. She blinked and he remained, combing his hair in front of what must be his dresser. There was a lamp, a wristwatch, a wallet, some bills and change, and three books on it and everything looked very real. She rubbed her eyes but the image didn't fade. Rather it seemed to gradually grow larger until it filled the picture frame.

The man stood quietly, dressed in a long-sleeved black polo and dark jeans. As she watched, she realized that he was truly gorgeous, wavy chestnut hair that curled over the neckband of his shirt, a truly perfect profile with a straight nose and beautiful lips. She couldn't quite make out the color of his eyes and finding out seemed important. She moved off the bed, but as soon as the angle changed, the image faded and all she could see was the original black-and-red abstract design.

"Dumb," she said out loud. "What nonsense."

Ellie wandered into her mini-kitchen, pulled a beer from the fridge, and filled a glass. She carried it back into the bedroom and again gazed at the painting. And that was what it was. A painting. Only a painting.

Stretched out on the bed again Ellie reached for the TV remote. When she glanced at the painting once more, it dissolved and the hunk was there again. Now he turned to face her, seeming to fumble for something. A TV remote. It was as though she was gazing at him from out of his TV.

She took a moment to admire his face. Classic lines, deep brown eyes, arching eyebrows, and a firm chin with a deep cleft. *God*, she thought, *he's really fabulous.* He had wide shoulders and beautiful hands, with long, graceful fingers.

Sipping her beer she followed his movements as he settled on his bed to watch TV. He made himself comfortable, feet facing her, and grabbed a beer from his bedside table. He sipped, and so did she. It was like sharing something.

Time slipped by and eventually he flipped off his TV and stood at the foot of his bed, giving her a great view of his well-developed physique. He grasped the back of his shirt and pulled it off over his head.

Great chest, she thought, *with lots of curly dark hair.* He had well-defined biceps and muscular shoulders. He unbuttoned his jeans, then turned and disappeared from view. Damn. Just when things were getting good. *Bathroom*, she thought. Tooth brushing and the like. It helped to control her developing lust to think of him doing mundane stuff like that.

He returned and, while she watched, almost drooling, unzipped and pulled off his jeans. He stood in all his glory, wearing only a pair of black briefs, with no doubt about the treasure beneath. He wasn't erect but he did fill out the front of those black briefs really well.

She knew she was panting but she controlled herself as best she could as he turned and gave her a great view of his butt. Wow, what a butt, firm ass cheeks that moved provocatively beneath his cotton shorts as he walked away. Then the light went out.

Shit, she thought. *I might just have to have more pepperoni pizza tomorrow night.*

Reluctantly she stood, removed her clothing and climbed into her bed, naked between the cool sheets. Just before she turned out the bedside light, she gazed at the painting, but it was again merely red-and-black swirls.

THE FOLLOWING EVENING SHE TRIED TO STAY IN THE LIVing room and resist the temptation to see whether Mr. Black Briefs was there again. *Hell*, she thought, *why resist?* She wandered into the bedroom and again stretched out on the bed. The painting dissolved and he was already there, this time in a kelly green shirt and chinos.

He was sooo hot. He absently combed his fingers

through those luscious waves and Ellie could almost feel the strands beneath her hands. Again time slipped by and soon he stood and turned off the TV. Had she spent an entire evening just watching him? He pulled off his shirt and she reached out, almost able to feel the smooth contours of his chest. Then he rubbed his palms over the exact spot her hands were reaching for and for a moment their fingers were superimposed.

Then slowly, sensually, his hands stroked down his belly, her hands following. It was as though he felt something more than just his palms and his eyes closed. He unbuttoned his jeans and her palms followed his over the thick line of hair that arrowed down from his navel. His pants slid to the floor and his palms cupped his balls through his black cotton briefs.

She was touching him. She couldn't deny it any longer. She actually felt him beneath her hands. How? She had no clue, but she was touching him. She knew it, and so did he. Ellie watched as his cock grew hard, making a delightfully enormous bulge beneath the dark fabric.

She kept one hand where it was, but slipped the other beneath her own khakis and found her mound. Her fingers rubbed her clit through her nylon panties. It was like mutual masturbation. He rubbed faster, and so did she.

Suddenly he pulled off his briefs and wrapped his fingers around his erection, stroking the length of him as she watched, and felt. She moved her hand beneath her panties and found her sopping clit.

She watched as his strokes got faster and his hips rolled. Then she saw semen erupt from his cock and cover his stroking hand. She came, too, waves of pleasure spearing through her.

Heart pounding, almost unable to breathe, Ellie closed her eyes and minutes later, when she opened them, the painting was back.

Disappointment filled her. He was gone. Would he be there the following evening? She almost wept.

THE NEXT MORNING SHE DRESSED IN FRONT OF HER PAINTING, then slowly walked out toward the bus stop. And there he was, standing, waiting. It was him! She was sure of it, same wavy chestnut hair, same body, a body she now knew so well. He turned and looked at her, but there was no spark of recognition. And why would there be?

"Good morning," he said, politely.

"Good morning." It was all she could do not to stutter.

"I'm new here. This is the stop for the number four bus, isn't it?" His voice was as sexy as she'd expected.

"It is. And welcome to the neighborhood."

He now looked at her fully. "Thanks. It seems like it's a pretty nice area. Do you take this bus every day?"

"Yes," she mumbled, unable to make her brain behave. "I'm Ellie."

"Nick," he said and extended his hand. "Maybe I'll see you again from time to time."

You sure will. I'll see to it. "Sure. That would be great."

Oh yeah, she thought. *Oh yeah!*

At the Office

〰✠〰

*A*NGELA WAS A DATA-ENTRY CLERK FOR A LARGE INDUS-
trial firm. That Friday afternoon she got a call from the guy
who was repairing her home computer, telling her it wouldn't
be ready until the middle of the following week. "Damn,"
she muttered when she hung up. She felt totally cut off from
the world when she couldn't get her email, and personal use
of the office machines was absolutely forbidden.

She looked at her watch then glanced around the office. It
was almost six and there was no one left at any of the desks.
Since it was after working hours, she decided that no one
would be monitoring computer use so she clicked over to her
email server. Along with several chatty letters from friends

and one from her sister, there were several notes forwarded from the site server, each with the same idea.

Hey, blue-eyed girl, how about another story? It's been much too long.

I miss your stories, blue.

You said you'd upload another tale this week. It's Friday. No story.

It was both flattering and frustrating. She wrote erotic short stories, good ones if the comments from readers were at all reliable. She usually uploaded at least one piece of erotic fiction each week, but since her computer had been sick she hadn't been able to. She'd carefully backed up all her completed tales onto a flash drive then deleted them from her hard drive. It would never do for the repair guys to read her hot, erotic fiction. What would they think of her? She had the drive in her wallet and she could upload any one of her tales, but from her office? Her manager would go ballistic if she ever found out. However . . .

What the hell. She took a deep breath then decided that she would log on from someone else's desk, pop in her flash drive, upload a story, and no one in the front office would ever be the wiser. Of course! It was the obvious solution.

She found the little drive in her purse and inserted it into the USB port on Madge's desktop in the next cubicle.

Clicking on Explore, she listed the drive's contents. Maybe "Jennie's Hot New Romance" for this week.

She logged on to the fiction site, entered the required user name and password, and began the process. As she watched the screen, she felt a hand on her shoulder. "Hey, Angela. What's going on? Personal stuff?"

She immediately recognized the voice. Harry Masters was one of her coworkers and they had been carrying on a light office flirtation for several weeks. She whirled around and tried not to look guilty. Harry was really cute, tousled curly brown hair, deep soulful eyes, and a nice warm grin that made dimples appear on either side of his mouth when he smiled, and he smiled often. And he was sexy as hell. Actually he was the fantasy inspiration for several of her pieces of fiction.

What could she say? "Yeah. My home computer is on the fritz. I didn't think anyone would mind."

"Why should anyone mind?" he said. "It's after business hours."

"Thanks," she said. "I'll only be a moment."

UPLOAD SUCCESSFUL—UPLOAD ANOTHER?

She moved to pull the flash drive from the port when Harry looked at her suspiciously and said, "What the hell is that? You're at Madge's computer. I hope you haven't put some kind of virus on the system."

"No, not at all," she said with a light laugh. "It's just a bit of fiction I put on a story site. Anyway the company antivirus software would catch anything bad. Don't worry."

He raised an inquisitive eyebrow. "I don't mean to seem overly intrusive, but I'm sure you realize how careful we have to be about viruses and spyware."

She grinned. "Of course, but it's nothing like that."

"I really don't want to tell anyone about this, but I don't want to lose my job if something bad happens." He slowly shook his head. "You've got to understand. The word *upload* scares the hell out of me. Exactly what did you just do?"

Embarrassed, Angela was reluctant to show Harry her story. "Like I said, it's just a short story. I write bits of fiction that a friend of mine posts on the web. Really, it's nothing that might harm the system."

His face softened. "That's great," he said. "Satisfy my curiosity. Let me glance at what you just did, and I'll be out of your way."

"See the story?"

"Sure. I like short stories."

Suddenly she felt her face flush and heat rise all over her body. "It's a little personal. Can't we just let it go?"

"Personal, huh?" His smile widened and he lightly stroked her cheek with his thumb. "Now I'm no longer as worried. Instead you've got me intrigued. What could it be that makes you so uncomfortable?"

Resigned, unable to get out of this situation without

showing Harry her story, she clicked on the message and the site upload page appeared. "See? Just a story."

"'Jennie's Hot New Romance,'" Harry read out loud. His laugh was warm and rich, flirtation back in his eyes. "An erotic story, perhaps?"

She couldn't keep her face from heating. "Sort of. Like the title says, romance and stuff."

"Good for you," Harry said. "I love a well-written piece of fiction, and I never knew we shared something like that. What site do you write for?"

She told him the name, hoping that he wouldn't realize the true nature of her tales. No such luck. His face brightened and his smile showed his even, white teeth.

"You write for that site? I love that collection," he said, now totally blowing her mind.

"You've been to the site? You read erotic short stories?"

"From time to time," he said, looking a bit abashed. "What's your screen name?"

Reluctantly, she said, "Blue-eyed girl."

"You've got to be kidding me. You wrote, 'Mandy's Honeymoon Night'?"

Her own smile widening, Angela said, "Sure. You read it?"

"What a small world." He thought, then said, "And 'Office Politics'?"

"Right again. I can't believe the coincidence. You read my stuff." She'd written "Office Politics" as a result of a vivid fantasy about Harry.

"Nice writing. I fantasized about that story a lot, and put you and me in it."

Her entire body heated. "You're joking."

"Not at all. When the couple did it on the conference table, I pictured you with your skirt around your waist and your naked pussy just waiting for me."

Angela swallowed hard. She'd had the same fantasy about him. She couldn't utter a single word.

He raised an inquisitive eyebrow. "Want to try it?"

"Don't be silly," she said. "We couldn't."

"Why not? The office is empty and the cleaning folks don't arrive until late. We're consenting adults, and we've been flirting for quite a while. I find you very attractive and I hope you find me at least passable."

"More than passable," she blurted out. "But . . ."

"I'm not usually into casual sex, but thinking about that story has made me curious, and I can tell you're turned on by it, too." He reached into his pocket, pulled out a condom, and waggled it in front of her eyes. "This way we will know before we start dating whether we're sexually compatible." He winked. "The story fits this situation. Let's not let this coincidence go to waste. Let's see whether it will work as well in reality as it did in your writing." He paused and, when she hesitated, he added, "Come on. Be a sport. What could it hurt?"

She couldn't help but laugh, amazed and charmed by his audacity. He reached out his hand and held it there. Slowly she raised her own and placed it in his.

"Conference table?" she asked as they walked down the hall.

"Right. Like in the story. Did you write that one from experience?"

"Of course not. I never did it in there." She looked down slightly shy. "Have you ever done it in there?"

Harry opened the door to the large room with its upholstered chairs and huge, highly polished table and almost dragged her inside. "Not until now."

He kissed her until she was feeling almost drugged, then he removed his jacket, tie, and white-on-white shirt, draping them over the chair at the end of the long, oval table. "This way it's like old man Jenkins is watching us."

Although he didn't have the bodybuilder physique she'd described in her story, there was little fat on him. Without another word, Harry unbuttoned her blouse and took it and her bra off. Angela stood a little straighter, hoping to expand her 34B breasts, praying that he'd like what he saw. From the expression on his face, she knew he did.

"Very nice," he said. "Very nice, indeed." She wanted to behave like the characters in her story did, acting bold and sure of themselves while undressing their partners, but she couldn't get her fingers to cooperate. She tried to unbuckle his belt with fumbling digits but he pushed her hands aside. "No need," he said. "This is a little new to me, too."

They kissed again for a short while, his kiss thorough, deep, and sexual, a prelude to what they'd agreed was to come.

He unzipped, unfastened, and unhooked both of them until they were completely naked. She looked him over, wide shoulders, well-defined waist, long legs sprinkled with light brown hair, pretty good build, and an average-size cock, not yet fully erect.

He grasped her around the waist and lifted her until she sat on the edge of the mahogany surface. It was cool and slippery beneath her cheeks.

He turned to the chair with his clothing over it. "How about this, Jenkins?" he said. "She's really lovely, isn't she? However, you can't have any. She's mine." Just when she began to think he'd taken this all a little too seriously, he added, "For right now at least."

He played with her breasts and nipples until she was gasping for air, then he leaned her back on the table. She barely noticed the cold, hard wood beneath her.

He grabbed the condom, unrolled it over his now-hard dick, and pulled her forward by the hips until her ass was at the very edge of the wooden surface. Then he found her opening, parted her inner lips, and slid his cock into her slippery channel. *God, he feels good*, she thought.

Slowly he withdrew then slid in again. After a few slow, smooth thrusts he lost control and began to ram into her, filling her to perfection. Then she began to slide backward across the slick wood. Realizing what was happening but too far gone to care, he grabbed her beneath her knees and she grasped the edge of the table, hanging on tightly.

Over and over he pounded into her until he came, hips pushed forward, grasping hands digging small furrows in her skin.

Eventually he pulled out and removed the condom. He gazed at her then smiled, wider and wider, until his rich, warm laugh filled the room. Although she was a bit sexually frustrated, she couldn't help joining him until their laughter echoed off the walls. It took a few long minutes until they both calmed. "I'm so sorry," he said when he'd caught his breath. "I got a little carried away and when I couldn't hold you still . . ." He chuckled again.

"I know and it's okay. In my story it was all so easy."

"It didn't live up to my expectations either. I know you didn't enjoy it nearly as much as I did."

"It's really all right."

"No, it's not, but we'll take care of that later. How about we have dinner together, then go back to my place where, on a nice soft bed, I can show you what a considerate lover I can be?"

She huffed out a breath. She loved it that he cared about her pleasure. "Sure." She rose and began to dress.

"Right. It will be our first date."

She laughed again. "I like that idea."